DRAGON'S DESIRE

RED PLANET DRAGONS OF TAJSS BOOK EIGHT

MIRANDA MARTIN

GRAB MIRANDA MARTIN'S NEWSLETTER AND BE THE FIRST TO KNOW ABOUT NEW RELEASES, DEALS AND GENERAL ANTICS

CONTENTS

BLURB

I'm a warrior with the soul of a dragon.
To protect my female, I'll kidnap her...

The devastation killed most of our population. Since then, Zmaj men have lived isolated and without females. That changed when a ship with human passengers crashed on our planet. For the first time in many years, we have females in our midst.

But some of the new humans fear our species. One of them, a quiet, dark-haired beauty with a fierce spirit, awakens my dragon. When I catch her scent, lust heats my blood.

Tajss is fraught with danger, not only from the scorching desert and blood-thirsty animals, but the battles among its peoples. Sarah doesn't see the threats that lurk in the shadows, but I do.

As second in command of the Tajss tribe, I face the choice of fulfilling my duty, or protecting Sarah. She's become my world. My mate. I'll keep her safe.

Even if it means kidnapping her...

Don't miss the beginning. It begins with Dragon's Baby and carries on from there!

PROLOGUE

SARAH

Seven Days after Gershom's Exile

"One more step, one more," Jackson mutters, struggling next to me.

Sweat pours down his bright red, blistering face, brow furrowed in concentration as he pushes forward. Two others struggle along with us, Tessa and Caleb, together the four of us forming the tail of Gershom's exiles.

It's been seven days since we left the safety of the city of Draconov and its dome. Seven days without epis, without a safe place to sleep, without hope.

Tessa stumbles and falls, crying out, arms pinwheeling. Jackson dives for her, but the sand holds him back, causing him to also fall. Caleb and I struggle over and help them to their feet.

"Thanks," Tessa says, shaking her head.

"No problem," I say, forcing a smile.

She dusts herself off, shakes her head, then her shoulders slump.

"Shit," Caleb exhales.

"What are we doing?" Jackson asks, raising and dropping his arms.

"Surviving," I answer.

"We shouldn't have followed him," Tessa says, desperation in her voice.

If she weren't dehydrated, I know tears would be streaming. Her soft brown hair is limp, heavy with sweat. Her once-pale face is burned and peeling, her lips cracked.

"We can't go on like this," Caleb says. "It's too..."

He trails off and I wait, hoping he'll say he wants to turn back. Please say it, Rosalind would welcome us back to the City.

"We need to move," Jackson says, filling the void before the words come.

"Yeah," Caleb sighs. "Yeah."

For the hundredth time, I swallow my disappointment, which feels like a mouthful of sand. We resume marching, but now we're sticking closer to one another. Short rations, lack of water, no epis, and sleeping fitfully on the sand with one eye open, sure that one of the many Tajss threats is going to kill me at any moment, all are taking their toll. Somewhere there's a limit, and I'm sure I'm going to reach it.

Ahead of us, hazy from the waves of heat rising from the sand, is the blurry outline of the rest of the exiles, marching on towards the horizon. Two days ago, Gershom gave a rousing speech about leading us back to our roots. We're returning to the wreckage of the generation ship. Our home, or what's left of it.

No matter how rousing his speech was, I knew it wasn't a good idea. The wreckage is exactly that, wreckage. The systems that made the ship a home are broken. There are no environmental controls. Because I secretly work for Rosalind, I know that there is power to parts of it still, but the things that made life on the ship normal are gone. The only good thing is that there were supplies left. Since we don't have any hunters, food and water are a first concern and the ship answers that.

It's a temporary fix, and I'm sure Gershom knows it.

It's not like I have a better idea.

March, Sarah. Keep up the pace, one foot then another.

"I miss vid sticks," Tessa pants.

"Did you see that rock thing Rosalind brought with her?" Caleb asks. "What the hell was that? It looked like something out of a superhero movie. Like one of those Marvel movies."

"Those monsters she brought with her are the only reason we're in this mess," Jackson huffs. "Everything was fine before she screwed it up, again."

"We were starving," I point out.

"So?" Jackson counters. "We had water! Food was being figured out. Gershom said he had a plan."

Of course he did. Gershom always has a plan, and you idiots believe him.

"Maybe," Tessa says, glancing quickly in my direction. Was that doubt in her eyes?

"New Doctor Who, or original?" Caleb asks, pointedly changing the conversation.

"New," I answer.

"Original," Jackson says.

"I prefer romances," Tessa says.

Jackson, walking slightly behind Tessa, opens his eyes wider at her comment and cracks a smile. "Yeah?" he prompts.

"Yeah," she says, but doesn't elaborate.

Me too, Tessa. Except my own romance is being screwed by your leader. I found my man. He's perfect, everything a girl could ever want. No romance book-cover model could compare. Huge, bulging arms, massive, muscled chest and abs, so tall, and strong, and forbidding, but so soft on the inside. A warmth I could cuddle in forever, wrapped in his arms. I didn't get to tell him goodbye or even talk to him about this whole jacked-up situation.

Thanks, Gershom. Dick.

An ache in my chest throbs with the beating of my heart. It's an emptiness with no way to fill it. All I can do is avoid it, focus on each moment, and push it aside. My only hope is that Calista was able to make him understand. I couldn't trust it with one of the Zmaj. He wouldn't have listened to any of the men. All the other Zmaj—the handful of natives to this desert planet who are literally dragon-men, complete with scales, horns, tails, and wings while still humanoid—have difficulty getting along. One of them telling another that his chosen has been exiled on a special mission wouldn't go over well.

Especially with Drosdan. All the Zmaj are big, huge in comparison to a human, and Drosdan is big in comparison to them. Six inches taller than any other Zmaj I've seen and twice as wide. He's so strong...

"But not romantic comedies?" Jackson is asking.

I've missed a chunk of conversation while lost in my thoughts.

"Not really," Tessa shakes her head.

"Hey, guys," Caleb says.

"So only, like, serious ones?" Jackson asks.

Tessa shrugs. "Sure, I guess, I don't know. What difference does it make? There aren't any anymore. All the vid sticks and players were destroyed in the crash."

"Guys," Caleb says again.

"I heard a rumor that there're still some working," Jackson says.

"Guys!" Caleb says, his voice cracking.

Three of us stop struggling forward and look at him.

"What?" three of us ask at once.

He's pointing back behind us, his arms shaking, his red face pale.

"What is that?" he asks, entire body trembling now.

Following his pointing arm, my stomach drops to the ground. It can't be...

Jackson shields his eyes with his hands, straining to see. I don't have to, I know, with absolute certainty, what that is.

Drosdan.

Elation mixes with fear. He's coming for me! My heart swells until it has to burst out of my chest, but it's tempered by the cold knot in my stomach. They can't see this. If they see me talking to him, they'll know I'm a spy. It will ruin everything. All of this will have been for nothing.

Drosdan is a blur. It looks like he's flying across the desert. Wings spread wide, arms pumping at his sides, racing with an ease and speed no human could ever hope to achieve. Every other step he leaps, gliding through the air, then hitting the ground running a few steps and repeating the motion.

"Run!" I scream.

I have to get them out of here.

Tessa and Jackson, eyes wide, spin and burst into a run. But Caleb is frozen in place. Fighting my way to him I slap him across the face.

"CALEB!" I scream, inches from him. "RUN!"

He jerks back, eyes clearing, shaking his head, mouth moving but no sounds emerging. I grab his shoulders, spin him around, and push. He stumbles, but it gets him moving. They crest the dune we were climbing and drop down the other side without looking back. Once they're out of sight I move towards Drosdan, closing the distance between us quickly, wholly thanks to him, my contribution is negligible.

"No," he says, sliding to a stop, sand spraying up.

"Drosdan—"

"NO!" he yells, raising his massive fists in the air. "No. No way. This can't be. They can't demand this, anything but this."

Overwhelming emotions war inside my body, too many to express. He's shaking, tail lashing back and forth throwing sand up. I can't form words, can't breathe, or move. Fighting past it, I move closer and place a hand on his chest. His arms wrap around me, pulling me tight.

All I want is to stay in his arms. Conforming my body to the hard muscles of his chest, resting my fingertips on his cool scales—this is where I belong.

Except for duty.

I owe Rosalind everything. She's right: we need these people. It's so much bigger than me, than Drosdan, bigger than us.

When she asked me to do this, my stomach hit the floor. All I could think about was Drosdan and what this would do to our budding relationship.

I didn't have a choice though, not really. Sure, Rosalind made it a choice, but she knew I would agree. I'd follow her into hell, and in a way, I almost literally have. Who else could do this? Gershom wouldn't let someone in his camp if he was sure they were tied to Rosalind. He probably suspects me, but I've always been helpful. So I said yes.

"I'm sorry," I say. "I have to."

Rising onto my toes I kiss him and pull away, fingertips lingering on his chest. I don't think Zmaj can cry, but the hurt on his face is a knife driving into my heart. The ache throbbing deep in my chest is too much. Stumbling back, breaking contact, I'm shaking, struggling to find words.

"Okay," he says, barely opening his mouth.

I'm not sure I heard him speak, or if I imagined it. A few feet separate us, but it might as well be miles. His wings droop, and his tail lies still on the sand. His eyes lock to mine, but neither of us can speak. I can't. It's too much. It hurts so bad.

I take one step backwards. Then another. He doesn't move, letting me go.

His shoulders drop further, his head lowers.

Another step. Muscles tremble with more than effort. Duty pushes but my heart is pushing back. We haven't had our chance yet. It's not fair!

Drosdan and I are still getting to know each other. There's been no time for us. No chance for anything—a few stolen kisses, a walk in the moonlight. I'm no Zmaj with some primal instinct for a treasure! I want to get to know him better, to make sure these feelings are real, that they're more than physical. This ache in my heart is more than infatuation. It's not right.

Rosalind has Visidion, why can't I have mine?

Responsibility. The survival of both our races.

He knows it as well as I do.

We do what we have to do.

"I'm sorry," I whisper.

"I'm sorry too," he says, shaking his head.

"We're going to the wreckage," I say. "Can you let them know?"

He nods slowly, head hanging low.

"There's a rock," he says. "Maybe half an hour's walk from there," he says. "It's big. Follow the second sun in the morning—you'll find it."

"Okay?" I ask, climbing the dune backwards still.

"I'll leave messages there," he says. "And food. I'll get food for you. Epis."

Relief floods through me. Epis withdrawal has been my biggest concern in this endeavor. I can't get caught taking it, even though I'm certain Gershom is himself. It would be another sign I'm a plant, and I have no idea what they would do then.

"Thank you," I say, another tear falling.

Drosdan nods, still as a rock watching my retreat. When I reach the top of the dune and turn, he's still standing, watching. My body locks. Emptiness aches inside. I can't do this. It hurts too much. A tremor starts in my left thigh, expanding until both legs are shaking. Tears fall, wasting precious water, and I raise an arm, stretching my hand towards him.

They won't survive without me. Tessa, Jackson, Caleb, all the other followers. Sad and misguided, yes, but they're not bad people. They follow Gershom out of fear, even if they don't see it yet. I'm their only hope of surviving. Follow my heart and they'll die. Certainty fills the emptiness, and I do what I have to do. Forcing myself, I turn away from Drosdan.

There will be time, a time for us. There has to be.

1

SARAH

"You can't be serious!" I exclaim, snapping my jaw shut to avoid getting sand in my mouth.

"What?" Jackson says.

The confusion on his face causes a pain deep inside my head. He doesn't get it. How, I can't begin to fathom, but he doesn't. Rubbing my temples, I close my eyes and focus on controlling the raging ball of fire inside me. The urge to scream at him until he gets it is so strong I can't speak. I know if I do it will all come ripping out and I will fillet him. No matter how nice that would be it won't accomplish anything.

"Sarah, it's an idea," Tessa interjects, shaking her head, brown hair floating around it like a halo. "How bad could it be?"

The throbbing pain in my head pulses, and I move my fingers to my eyes in hopes of keeping them from exploding.

"Look," I say, continuing to massage my forehead while holding my eyes in. "It is a bad idea. No, it's not bad, it's terrible, or... whatever is worse than that!"

My voice cracks at the end from the strain of not

screaming at them. Why did I agree to do this? Rosalind be damned, I don't want to be here. I'm burning up, tired, and hungry, none of which is making it easier to deal with these people.

"But if we do that we'd have food for a month, maybe two!" Jackson exclaims.

Shaking my head, I sigh and open my eyes. Jackson stares at me, earnest. He's not a bad guy, topping six feet with an average build, and he has a nice face. I know he's doing his best, but he's not a survivor. On the generation ship, before we crashed here on Tajss, he was an office worker. Did something with data input, a specialist in computer stuff.

None of us were prepared to face life on Tajss. How do you prepare to survive on a barren desert planet? We were supposed to live our lives on the ship. It wasn't supposed to reach its destination until long after we were gone. My great grandkids or their grandkids, I don't even remember. It wasn't important then and it's less so now. We're not on the nicely terra-formed planet that was sitting out there ready for us, which would have been a small transition from life on the ship.

Tajss is a beast of its own. Two red suns beat down on it, and everything is out to kill you. Literally everything, even the damn plants will try to kill you if you don't know what you're dealing with. Rolling sand dunes for as far as the eye can see, broken only by occasional rocky protrusions. A lot of my friends like to debate if it's more like Tatooine or Vulcan, except Jolie. She thinks it's more like Gallifrey, but she's the main Whovian survivor and an outlier in her opinion.

Fun times, debating the merits of the theories. Back when I was with my friends, before I agreed to be Rosalind's spy in with those who followed Gershom into exile. It's been a month, maybe a little more, and things are going from bad to worse.

In order to survive here on Tajss, humans need to take a plant called epis. I don't know exactly what it does, but somehow it adjusts our bodies to tolerate the extreme heat. Trouble is that it's hard to get, doesn't last long once harvested, and oh yeah, I'm in Gershom's "Humans First" camp of exiles who all proudly refuse to have anything to do with the local aliens, the Zmaj.

As if we have any right to refuse them. It's their damn planet! The Zmaj are the survivors of the alien race that inhabited this planet. They're like dragon-men, tall, strong, covered in scales complete with wings and tails and horns. They're sexy too, if you like that kind of thing, and what can I say, I do. The first Zmaj the survivors met fell in love with my friend Calista and led us to his City. That's where all of us were living before Gershom's exile. A nice city with a sparkling force field dome that cut down the heat a lot and kept the random dangerous animals out. It was great.

Except Gershom is a tool. He made a power grab against my boss, Lady General Rosalind, and long story short, he lost. She exiled him and anyone else who wanted to follow his bullshit ideas of "Humans First" and "reject the alien threat" rhetoric. Rosalind is smart though, she doesn't want him out here scheming without keeping an eye on him. Hence, she asked me to be her plant in his camp.

It's not easy though. They don't take epis so the heat is killing them, literally. Dehydration is a quiet killer, sapping your strength, causing havoc in your body. Because he had no place to go, Gershom led the couple of hundred who decided to follow him to the piece of the generation ship we got here in. It's the only shelter any of us know about besides the City. I guess we could have gone to the Tribe, a group of Zmaj who showed up later, but then he'd have to get help from Zmaj, not to mention they hate him and would probably kill him on sight.

So here we are, living in the wreckage of our former ship, struggling for the necessities of life. There are supplies left on the ship but not enough for the long haul, and they've already been put on rations. We get enough salt and potassium to keep us from dying, but not enough to feel good. Food is also a problem. The rations that came down with the ship were taken with us when we left here, following Ladon to his City.

The Zmaj are hunters. A few reasonable humans have learned to hunt under their guidance. That, of course, is out of the question for this group. Learn from a Zmaj? Oh no no, thank you, we're human, and we don't need no stupid lizard teaching us anything.

"Okay, look," I say, forcing calm into my voice, but my stomach is churning, and the hair on my arms stands on end. "First, what cliff are you planning on herding the stampede over?"

Jackson's eyes widen, his shoulders slump, then his eyes light up and he opens his mouth to speak but I hold up a hand cutting him off.

"Wait," I say, shaking my finger in his face. "Assuming you have a cliff, how do you start this stampede?"

"Oh that's easy, we get behind the herd of bivo, and we tag one of them with a low power zap from the energy guns."

It hurts, physically hurts to listen to him. The stupidity of it is literally painful.

"Right…" I say, shaking my head trying to comprehend why he can't see how terrible this idea is.

"Yeah, if you startle one of them, then the rest will react too! Then they run and we just wait for them to go over the cliff. Then we harvest the meat and fur!"

He bounces with excitement. Desperate, I look to Tessa

for support, but she's grinning too. Obviously she thinks this idea is brilliant. Great.

"You realize the entire problem is that the bivo don't notice when we hit them with a full blast from the energy guns, right?"

"Sure, but that's why this works! We're not trying to kill one, all we do is startle the herd then let them run," he answers.

"How do you make sure they're heading in the right direction?" I ask, struggling to not roll my eyes.

"We put people on either side of the herd," he answers, straightening his shoulders and grinning.

"Okay, so people on either side of a herd of what, twenty to thirty bivo? Each one weighing around four to five hundred pounds?"

"Yeah," he says, nodding.

"And if they get off course a bit, these people... shout at them? Or shoot them?"

"Shoot them," he says, nodding faster.

"With the energy guns," I say.

"Yeah!" he says, bouncing again while nodding even faster.

"The same guns we already established don't affect the bivo," I say. "The jolt doesn't get past their hides."

"Rig-" he starts, then it hits him and he stops. His shoulders slump. "Oh."

Tessa is as crestfallen as he is. A hard knot forms in my stomach seeing them. They're not bad people. Desperate, maybe a bit stupid, but not bad people. That's my problem with this entire situation. None of Gershom's "followers" are bad people, or the majority aren't. They're scared, confused, and lost.

"It's okay," I say, putting a hand on Jackson's shoulder. "I'm hungry too."

"It seemed like a good idea," he says, his stomach grumbling loudly.

"Yeah," I say. "It's too dangerous, is all. We've already lost two hunters, we can't afford to lose any more."

"Right," he agrees.

"I'll see what I can do," I say. "I did some work with the hunters back in the city. I think I can get us some food."

Both of their eyes light up.

"Great!" they say together, then look at each other and laugh.

The chemistry between the two of them is as obvious as the double suns in the sky, but I don't think Jackson is getting the message that she's as interested as he is. He looks away from Tessa quickly. She frowns, her brow furrowing, her long brown hair drifting around her face in the hot breeze. Well, here is something I might be able to do that's helpful.

"Hey, Jackson," I say.

"Yeah?" he asks, kicking his foot through the sand.

"Could you and Tessa go up into the old medical bay of the ship and sort through those boxes?"

"Huh?" he asks, looking at me and frowning.

Darting my eyes at Tessa then back, I frown, trying to will him to get it. Her eyes are dancing with excitement—she gets it at least.

"It's really hard to get into there," he says.

"I know, that's why I asked both of you to do it," I say.

"Oh, man," he grouses, kicking the sand in my direction.

"Because you two would be alone, and it could take a while," I say, going blatant on it.

"Alo—" he stops mid-word, eyes widening. A slow grin spreads across his face. "Yeah, of course."

He glances at Tessa, and I swear I can see his heart pounding in his chest. The beads of sweat rolling down his face are from much more than the heat alone. Tessa smiles, meeting his eyes, then the two of them walk off together.

Well, one good deed for the day done.

I turn back towards the wreckage we're calling home, and a soft, hot breeze stirs the sand and cools my sweat. People move listlessly around the ship, sticking mostly to the shade. The wreckage is massive, like a giant splinter stuck into the sand and rising hundreds of feet into the sky. It's hard to comprehend that this is only a small section of the ship that used to be our home. Inside it was just home, and only a very few of us had an opportunity to see it from the outside. The scope of it was massive. A testament to the will of humans and their desire to conquer the universe.

Or our innate desire to get rid of what we don't want. The vid sticks and our schooling painted a glowing picture of why the generation ships were built. Humanity reaching for the stars! Conquering the universe as we spread our wings and fly!

That's what they wanted everyone to believe but there was a lot more to the truth. It was all a big PR campaign. Our ancestors who chose to go on the ships did so to escape a life of poverty and hopelessness. Earth was overpopulated and only growing worse. There weren't enough resources to support the population and predictions were that by the next generation they wouldn't be able to feed everyone.

Too often there is more going on than what we see. Thank you, Rosalind for teaching me to open my eyes.

I've learned so much from her. Observation of what's really there, not what I want to be there. That one trait has served me well.

Sighing, I notice my awareness returning to the empty ache in my stomach. It consumes my motivation. Duty wars with desire. I don't want to be here, but I have to be. Rosalind asked, and I can't turn away from it. She needs to know when, not if, Gershom becomes a threat again. It's not for her, it's for the survival of two races, both human and Zmaj. I'm one of the few she's entrusted with her vision of the future. The merging of our two races into one new one.

There are no Zmaj females. They all died in the event they call the Devastation, the war that destroyed the planet, decades back. There aren't enough humans to make sure we're viable, and our bodies, even with the epis, aren't well adapted to the environment. I don't know when she came up with the plan, probably after Calista, a human survivor, and Ladon, the first Zmaj we met, hooked up, but more likely after Calista had their baby. The first crossbreeding of our two species. Illadon is cute as a button and mischievous as hell. He's also proof of the compatibility between us, with distinctly human and Zmaj traits both combined into something new.

As more humans and Zmaj have fallen for each other, the viability of that future became real. Why no one else is seeing it, I don't know, but if I had to guess, it's because surviving every day is enough of a pain in the ass for most of us. Rosalind thinks into the future. Lady General of the Generation Ship, she was in charge of the marines and pilots. Now, she's the de facto leader of the human race.

And she trusts me. She needs me here, and so I am. Away from my friends and the one male I'm interested in. Does Rosalind know?

My brow furrows. Does she? She has an almost magical ability to know things, but I don't think she does. How could she? It's not like Drosdan and I have made any public announcements or displays of our affection. He's Visidion's, the leader of the Tribe, second in command. He's as loaded up with duty as much as I am, every bit as loyal and dedicated too. And big, even for a Zmaj, who are huge, he's big. Twice the size of the rest of the Zmaj males. When he wraps his massive arms around me, encompassing me, I melt into him. Nothing has ever made me feel so... safe.

In public, with everyone else, he's rough and rude, but in the few moments we've managed to steal alone, he's gentle and soft. He's also the only reason this camp is still alive. He's been leaving food and epis for me at our secret rendezvous.

Warmth rushes out of my core and through my limbs. I turn my back on the camp in case anyone is looking. I don't want them to see the tears welling. It's all I can do to hold them in. I miss him so much. Inside, duty wars with desire, but in the end, duty wins out. It's not for me or Rosalind, it's for all of us. Rosalind is adamant that this group has to survive too, no matter how stupid their leader is. There's no way they'll make it on their own.

Right, here I am. Great.

The empty, rolling dunes, striated in shades of red and white accents, roll out before me all the way to the horizon. Empty and barren as I feel inside. Alone. I wish he was here or I was there with him. Sighing, I turn, tearing my eyes away while pushing the ache down, and return to the camp.

I don't know how long this can go on. Somehow, some-way, all these people need to figure out that they should go back to the City. How do I get them to overcome their fear?

2

DROSDAN

"I told him if he did that again I was going to knock his face in," Padraig says, crossing his bulging arms over his chest.

The blacksmith's deep voice grates on my nerves. Nothing is ever easy, especially with him. He's always ready to fight, with or without a reason. He's always used his size to intimidate others, but that doesn't work with me, and he knows it. Big as he is, I'm almost twice his size. He only tried it with me once. I put him on the ground so fast that he hasn't forgotten which of us is dominant—though he still pushes my buttons every chance he gets.

"How was I supposed to know?" Errol asks.

It's hard to understand what he's saying. Padraig landed at least one good hit, maybe more, and Errol's face is swelling.

"Because you shouldn't touch what doesn't belong to you!" Padraig roars, hands balling into fists.

"Enough," I say, not raising my voice.

Padraig shakes with anger but doesn't follow through

with the threat his posture implies. Visidion can't come home soon enough. Dealing with things like this is his strong suit, not mine. I'm no leader, I'm the second. That's what I want to be, working for him, not ruling in his stead.

"Drosdan," Errol says,

"I said enough," I hiss, dropping my arms. "You're in the wrong and you know it. Padraig, you're no better."

"I didn-" Padraig starts, but I cut him off with a glare.

"You can't beat up anyone who pisses you off," I say, fighting the desire to do it myself. "That's it. Now, both of you—get back to work."

They glare at each other, and then Errol shakes his head and leaves. Padraig continues staring. I wait. Is he going to try it? Tingles run down my arms to the tips of my fingers. Yes, Padraig, try it. Beating you down here in front of everyone would give me an incredible amount of satisfaction. Matching his glare with my own, waiting, please do it. Visidion can't be pissed if I'm ending a fight. Everyone in the camp would appreciate me giving you a solid beating. Hell, they'd probably all thank me. You've been on a rampage for a while.

His hand tightens into a ball—he's going to do it. The bijass, primal urges threatening to revert me to base instinct, the bijass rising feels good.

Excitement builds, a vibration runs through me. Outwardly I don't give him a sign. Let him think I'm not ready.

The muscles of his right arm tense, his jaw tightens, his tail rises, yes!

He spins on one foot and stomps away.

Damn it!

Some of the tension drains out of my back muscles. If only he had gone for it, I could have taken out some of my

19

frustrations on him. I roll my shoulders before I make my rounds, but the tension I carry in them won't let go.

Several females are working the garden. I pass them and enter the cool cavern, making my way deep into it past the farming efforts until I reach the crevasse that leads to where the epis grows. If Errol hadn't been working to widen the passage I'd never make it through. Scraping my wings against the stone as I squeeze through it sideways, I emerge on the other side. The long strands of softly glowing blue epis hang from the ceiling.

There's not enough here. The humans' need for it is endless, and it's not growing back fast enough. We're going to need a new source soon.

Another problem. I sent Samil to the City so that Visidion and Rosalind would be aware, but he hasn't returned yet. Finishing my count of the epis—how many are ready for harvest, how many for propagation—I squeeze back out.

When I emerge from the cavern, the suns' warmth hits my scales. More of my tension eases. The cool air of the cave is miserable, but the humans seem to enjoy it. They spend as much time in there as they can.

"Drosdan," Melchior calls.

"Yeah?" I ask, spotting the Zmaj hunter next to the wall, I join him.

The wall is almost finished. Ten feet tall, curving around and blocking off our area. No one has figured out a way to block the opening through it yet but I'm sure Padraig will figure out a solution, sooner or later.

Errol is constructing an arch over the opening today. There's a complex array of ropes, pulleys, and stacks of stone holding up other stones. It looks impractical but Errol is happy with the work. Penelope, the tall human female, watches the work, sharp green eyes flashing in the sunlight.

"You have to make sure that is stable before you add the

next stone," Penelope says, pointing up to where Errol is perched precariously on a makeshift ladder.

He shifts the stone he's working on, scraping it across the stack of stone that is holding it in the air.

"Better?" Errol asks.

"Yes," Penelope says. "I think so."

"We'll be leaving tomorrow," Melchior says.

"How long?" I ask, watching the ongoing work.

"Four, maybe five days," he says.

"Sounds good," I answer.

Leaning against the rock of the wall I watch the sand shift across the dunes. As soon as the two red suns go below the horizon, I'll be able to slip away. She's out there, waiting.

"You all right?" Melchior asks.

"Huh? Of course I am," I growl. "Wish Visidion would get his tail back here. I don't want to deal with this shit."

Melchior laughs and claps a hand on my shoulder.

"Yeah, I don't envy you," he agrees. "Herding majmun would be easier."

"Right," I agree.

"It's better, though," Melchior adds.

"What is?"

"Everything," he shrugs, shaking his head. "Better than it was."

"We were fine in the valley," I reply. "We had everything we needed."

"Except them," Melchior responds, looking over his shoulder to the females working the garden.

Red-hot anger flashes through me, consuming thought. Muscles tense, and my tail stiffens, rising behind me.

"Right," I hiss, refusing to look at the females.

"Hey, what?" he asks, his eyes widening as he takes a step back.

The fog of the bijass encompasses everything, clouding

my vision with the haze of pulsing frustration. These aren't the females I want. Mine was sent away by Rosalind, and Visidion allowed it, forcing me to stay here.

Melchior's shoulders drop, his hands come up before him, defensive, his tail stiffens.

Edicts. They guide us, rules laid down to keep us from losing ourselves to the bijass. I am myself. It's difficult to contain my anger. Damn it, Visidion, I shouldn't be doing this.

"I'm fine," I say, tail dropping to the hot sand.

"Right," Melchior says.

I glare at him and then turn on my heel. Ropes creak, a loud groan, then something snaps.

"Look out!" Errol screams.

"No!" Melchior hisses.

Chills run across my body, turning back as chaotic sound explodes. Screams, stone, cracks and booms crashing.

Melchior flies through the air, wings spread wide as he dives towards Penelope. Penelope is screaming, a high-pitched screech tearing at my ears unrelentingly. Errol is off the ladder going backwards, and the massive stone he was moving into place is falling. The ropes have broken.

It's a frozen tableau. Stomach dropping, I push forward and everything before me moves at the same time. Melchior's hand pushes Penelope, forcing her back. She stumbles, arms pinwheeling backwards. Errol is dropping slower than the stone. Melchior lands on his left shoulder, slamming into the ground. Ropes pile up around him, the stone closing on him.

I'm not going to make it.

I leap, spreading my wings, catching a draft of air.

The stone drops towards Melchior's head. I have to reach him. I can't fail.

Melchior rolls to the side, trying to get clear, but Errol falls in the way, blocking him as the two males collide.

I glide across the distance and slam to the ground under the stone as it drops. The weight of it strains my muscles. They scream with pain in response as I lift. The stone is slick and my fingers slip, I can't get a grip.

"MOVE!" I scream.

Can't lose my grip, have to keep it up. *Lift, damn it, lift!*

My knees tremble as I fight to keep it up. The stone weighs three or four times as much as I do. Melchior and Errol scrabble around each other, trying to get clear as the rock slips further. I can't hold it.

My back spasms. Pulling up, I shift my position and get my knees underneath myself but I can't hold it much longer. Muscles trembling, I focus on breathing through the pain. A tremble rips through me.

"CLEAR!" Melchior yells.

I glance left and right through slitted eyes, then push the rock up and away. It falls to the ground and thuds.

"Holy shit," Penelope exclaims.

"Damn," Melchior says, placing a hand on my shoulder. "Are you okay?"

Panting, hands on thighs, I glance at him, fighting the urge to punch him in the mouth for such a stupid question.

"Do I look okay?" I hiss.

The ground beneath our feet jumps.

"I'm sorry," Errol says. "I thought the—"

"Shh!" Melchior cuts him off, eyes widening as the ground trembles then jumps again.

Ah, damn it, I thought it was more of the stones falling.

"Wha—" Penelope starts, but Melchior places a hand over her mouth.

Straightening myself and looking around, I watch as the loose top layer of sand dances, bouncing up and down as the trembling of the ground increases. Noise, too much noise.

The females working the garden chattering, Padraig clanging metal into shape.

"QUIET!" I scream over my shoulder.

The ground behind me explodes, dirt showering down, and the scream of a zemlja echoes off the cliff walls.

3

SARAH

*S*noring and shifting bodies create a white-noise effect.

Slipping out of the room I share with five other girls, I lower myself out of the door and out into what was a hallway. Keeping close to the wall, I creep my way along, pausing every other step to listen for anyone coming.

I need to use the bathroom. That's my excuse if one of the handful of people on guard duty sees me.

Why don't you use the buckets we set up in each room? They'll ask me. I don't want to wake up my roommates. I respond. Oh, that makes perfect sense. What a nice person you are, they respond.

Okay Sarah, stop running the scenario in your head. You've got this. Also, stop referring to yourself in the third person. That's weird. Right, okay.

Is it bad I'm mentally talking to myself? Better than focusing on how hard my heart is beating right now. Or the cold beads of sweat running down my back despite the fact that it must be close to one hundred ten or twenty degrees, even now that the suns are down for the night.

I could be crazy. Good job, Sarah, psychoanalyze yourself while you sneak out in the middle of the night. Brilliant idea, I love it.

Footsteps echo off the metal walls of the crashed ship, and I freeze, pressing hard against the wall. My heart pounds hard in my chest. I'm dizzy. All my brilliant excuses for being out now are gone, I can't remember a single one of them.

The steps move closer. Crouching lower I imagine the shadows covering me like a blanket hiding me from sight. Bathroom. Bathroom. That's all, need the bathroom. Perfectly sensible.

Unable to breathe, the steps are right behind me, a metal wall dividing us. A cough, a shuffle, and then they move on. Eyes closed tight, I count. One, two, still going away, three, four. When I get to ten, I can't hear them any longer. Held breath explodes out of me, and I gasp in fresh air. The pounding in my chest slowly returns to normal. Sliding the rest of the way outside the ship, I don't encounter anyone else.

While Gershom insists that guards be on duty, which I give him credit for, those who draw the duty don't want to do it. The entire camp is apathetic about everything. They have no idea that the only reason they're eating right now is because of Drosdan and me. Well Drosdan, really. He's left meat for us that I conveniently 'find' and bring back to camp. Either none of them have thought to ask how I can keep getting so lucky finding dead bivo, or else they don't want to rock the boat by asking.

Gershom has given me a look a few times, but that's it. He must know that without my 'luck,' his camp would starve. Running across the open sand as fast as I can, the hair on my arms stands on end. Adrenaline pumps through my body. Being outside at night is scary as hell. The sismis hunt at night, roving packs of flying bat-like creatures big enough to take down a bivo, the large herd animals that roam the dunes. They let out a screech warning of an impending attack, but it's not like there is someplace I can hide if I'm targeted.

The area around where our section of the generation ship crashed is empty, rolling dunes. A few rocks jut out of the ground here and there, but nothing that would provide any protection. So far I've been lucky.

It doesn't matter. I'll see him soon. He'll protect me.

His bulging arms and gentle strength will wrap around me, pulling me tight against the hard muscles of his chest. His cool scales against my cheek. His fingers in my hair. My core tightens in anticipation.

We haven't actually done it, yet. The opportunity hasn't been there for us. I know I'm his treasure, he wants me to be his forever, but we haven't found a way to make it work yet. Duty is always in the way. His or mine.

I'm first to arrive at the rock protrusion we had worked out to be a drop spot, so I sit with my back against it. The moon is high in the clear sky, casting its silver glow across the rolling sand. Leaning back, I stare up at the stars twinkling brightly above. Rosalind has been out there now and brought back more aliens with her. I saw them from a distance but didn't meet them. It's hard to keep my cover with Gershom, so I couldn't get away.

What else is out there? Who else?

My thoughts wander as the stars turn in the sky. The hours pass by. I rise and turn a slow circle, hoping to see Drosdan approaching. It's not like him to miss a rendezvous. Emptiness forms in my stomach, pulsing with loneliness. Is he okay? What could keep him away?

Doing my best to push aside those thoughts, I gather a few small pieces of rock and form a circle. Inside the circle I draw a heart. It's crude, but enough. He'll know I was here as long as nothing happens to it. If someone else does come across it, it's not like they could trace it to me specifically.

A dim glow is forming on the horizon telling me I'm out of time. I look around one last time before I give up and jog for the ship.

4

DROSDAN

*T*he wall trembles. The zemlja climbs into the sky, thirty feet or more into the air, undulating its body, massive mouth opening to reveal the concentric rows of teeth going down its gullet.

Females scream behind me and the males close by hiss. I'm unarmed and can do nothing against the zemlja. Melchior grabs his lochaber off his back, whirling the bladed staff in one hand as he races towards the deadly worm. Errol grabs for Penelope.

I run towards the monster. A massive hammer Errol uses to shape stone lies on a table, so I grab it as I pass. The zemlja leans back, screaming, about to throw itself forward. They hunt by sound, so it will throw itself at the loudest noise and eat whatever it lands on.

If it does, the wall we've worked so hard to build will be destroyed, and it's so big it will likely land in the middle of the garden, with all our human females. The red suns rest on the horizon behind its monstrous body. I have only moments before it moves.

"Melchior!" I yell, pointing to the far side of the worm.

He nods and changes directions. We both spread our wings, bounding across the distance between us and the thing's body. Swinging the hammer one-handed, I put everything I have into it, slamming the massive head of the weapon into the worm.

The hard scales that protect it reverberate with the force of my blow. Numbing vibrations race up my arm to my shoulder. A web of cracks appears at the point of impact and the zemlja scream reaches a new pitch. Its body twists then retreats, sliding down into the ground.

Melchior slices at it with his lochaber but the blade slides across the scales, not finding purchase.

"Don't let it get below," I yell.

Melchior glares at the zemlja, swinging his lochaber again. As the body of the zemlja slides back into the hole it burst out of, I slam it over and over with the hammer. A shadow falls on me. High, high above me the monster's end is bent towards me, open maw plunging down.

I leap to the left. Its jaws snap shut, catching my tail.

Pain erupts, a wildfire of sensation racing through my body, then I'm ripped into the air. Twisting, desperate, I turn towards the zemlja and try to grab on. My fingers slide across its scales, not finding purchase. The ground races up. It's dragging me under. Can't let that happen.

Bending in half, the pain in my tail increasing as I struggle, I lift myself up and slide my fingers into its maw. The maw is five different parts that open or close, but with my tail stuck in it, there is a gap for me to get a grip.

Grabbing two sides, I pull it apart, trying to force it open.

Muscles straining, it seems impossible. Harder, willing the damn thing to open, I strain with all I've got.

"DROSDAN!" Melchior yells, but I focus.

No attention to spare, have to get free.

Sarah is waiting. Her sweet, soft face fills my thoughts,

and with it comes the rage. Pulling the bijass around me, I give myself to it. Anger, rage, the pounding demand to dominate. Nothing will best me.

"RAHRR!" I scream, pulling with everything I have.

The mouth moves, barely, but the thing adjusts its bite, and that's the opening I need. Roaring, I pull, forcing its mouth open and there's a ripping sound. The lower lip I was holding onto tears, hanging limp. My tail drops out, blood dripping, but free. The zemlja bucks, throwing itself forward then back. It costs me my grip, tossing me off. I'm flying through the air, wings spreading to slow my drop, but I'm tumbling head over heels. Wings catch the breeze, stopping the circular motion, but I drop to the ground like a stone.

Slamming into the ground, sand in my mouth and eyes, I roll to ease the impact. Coming to a stop, I spin and jump to my feet.

Melchior slices at the zemlja over and over, sharp blade glinting in the setting suns as it twirls around his head, cutting across. It's ineffective, unable to penetrate the thick scales, barely scratching the surface.

Behind him, the wall we've worked so hard to build is crumbling as the zemlja undulates sending shock waves through the ground. The monster screams, a high-pitched sound that cuts through my thoughts. Pain explodes in my head, driving me to my knees. The worm waves back and forth, circling—something is about to happen.

Time slows to a crawl. Melchior's blade slices through the air, moving an inch at a time. The zemlja leans back, its long, thick body blocking out the sun.

"MOVE!" I scream at Melchior.

The words come out of my mouth too slow. The zemlja flings forward, time speeds up, Melchior looks up, eyes widening. His blade hits, making a resounding ringing echoing. He leaps, but it's too late. The zemlja slams down, crushing him beneath its weight. Sand explodes into the air, blocking my vision. Leaping to my feet, I race into the cloud, my outer lenses snapping shut to keep the dirt out of my eyes.

Still can't see. Slithering sounds, a muffled groan, and the thing is going back underground. I have to find Melchior. A cold ball of ice forms in my guts sending chills through my limbs. He has to be alive.

"Melchior!" I scream.

I can't lose him. Holding my hands out I try to navigate to him by feel. The swirling sand from the zemlja fall continues. I strain my hearing for any signs of him but there's nothing. Finally, my foot touches something. Kneeling and feeling blindly around, I find him. Melchior groans and tension drains from my muscles. I run my hands over him, fumbling blindly until I find his shoulders. Getting a solid grip, I pull hard and drag him away from the cloud of sand and dust. My lungs scream for air, but I can't breathe, I'd only inhale sand and dirt. Dragging Melchior backwards towards what I think is the wall, I listen for the sounds of another attack. Silence lays heavy across the land. Did we drive it away?

A rock catches my foot, tripping me. Losing my grip on Melchior he drops to the ground as I stumbling clear of the cloud. Reaching into it, I grab Melchior and pull him out too. A trickle of blood runs out of his mouth, but his chest rises. He's breathing at least.

The cloud of sand and dust swirls as I retreat, pulling Melchior's limp form with me. The ground trembles and jumps. I leap backwards, jerking my friend with me. There's a rumbling and then a scream as the zemlja bursts into the air again. I can't fight it without leaving Melchior in harm's way. Tightening my grip on his shoulders, I pull up, throwing him into the air. Ducking under his limp form, I pull him onto my shoulders, turn and run.

The zemlja roars before diving back under the earth behind me. Running as fast as I can, unable to open my wings for extra lift because Melchior lies across them, my pace is slower than it could be. The wall looms before me. Ragnar is coming, along with Padraig and Bashir. The three males wave, motioning frantically behind me.

"DUCK!" Ragnar yells.

Instinct takes over, and I duck without thinking. The zemlja whooshes over my head, swinging its body blindly around. I've hurt it, but it's not giving up. Looking ahead, it's too close to the wall and our home. I have to get it further out into the open desert, away from our people. Crouching, I lay Melchior on the ground, spinning back towards the zemlja and sprinting at it.

"Follow me!" I yell, just to make noise and grab its attention.

Crouching low as it swings its massive body over my head, I run, stomping my feet as hard as I can. Zemlja hunt by sound; if I'm loud enough it will chase me. The ground beneath my feet rumbles. It's working.

Straightening, I run faster, spreading my wings to ease my way across the soft sand. As my right foot contacts the earth, the ground jumps up to meet me, causing me to hit more forcefully. Painful shock waves race up to my knee, and it tries to give way, causing me to stumble. I'm struggling to regain my balance when the ground bucks again, and I'm thrown back into the air. The scream of the zemlja fills my ears as it explodes out of the ground behind me.

Tucking my head down, I fold my wings and pull my tail tight, hitting the ground on my shoulder and rolling to lessen the impact, but I hit hard. Something snaps in my shoulder. Pain explodes and the bijass takes over. Anger, white hot, out of control. Roaring my rage and leaping to my feet, I turn to face the monster. Its shadow falls over me, blocking out the suns. It is thirty feet or more in the air, waving in a circle, then it bends over.

Its open maw, hundreds of sharp teeth in concentric circles, catch the suns' rays glinting. It slams down, fast. Holding my arms wide I welcome it. Reaching up, I grab the sides of its mouth. The impact drives me down into the sand. My knees scream in pain but hold. It pushes down, all of its weight, but I will not yield. Sarah is waiting for me. My treasure needs me. I will not be defeated by this creature.

The thing's jaws try to close. Screaming, I hold them open, pushing back against it. Muscles trembling, pouring everything I have into defeating it, I push it back, inches only. Digging deeper, muscles straining, I push outward. Its breath chokes me, hard to breathe, have to hold it back.

Melchior, Ragnar, Padraig, and Bashir appear in the corners of my red-hazed vision. They attack the creature with their lochabers. It screams, pulling back, but now I pull it to me, blocking its retreat.

Sharp blades drive between its scales, finding the soft flesh underneath. It jerks up, pulling with all it has, I try to hold it down, but I'm lifted off my feet into the air, gripping tighter, forcing it to keep its mouth open. It won't go underground as long as it's open. Even a zemlja has to breathe.

Whipping back and forth, it tries to shake me off. Shoulder muscles strain with the force. Suddenly it straightens, stopping its writhing. I'm balanced over its open mouth, holding onto its jaws on either side. The suddenness of the stop takes me by surprise and I drop into its maw.

Damn it. Bracing my feet against the other side I force it to keep its mouth open while also avoiding the drop into its gullet. I will not be eaten today!

"SARAH!" I scream, straining.

Her perfect face drifts before my mind's eye. She's waiting. I can't miss this chance to see her.

Damn you monster, I will win!

Pushing out, pouring all I have into it, the jaws strain to close, but I won't be defeated. It jerks, spasms running up through its long body. Slime and saliva make finding purchase hard. Struggling to keep a grip, I slide deeper. Sharp teeth shred my shoes, cutting my feet and hands.

The sky above shifts, then the thing is falling, and I'm along for the ride, holding my place between the concentric rows of teeth. It hits the ground, and I bounce around inside its mouth, gathering cuts and bruises. Losing my grip, the mouth falls shut but nothing happens.

"Drosdan!" Ragnar yells.

I hear them outside the thing, sounds of shifting and grunts of straining.

"Yeah," I say, taking a deep breath as the bijass retreats.

The anger fades with it, leaving behind cold emptiness. The rage is warm and easy, it pushes through, and I understand it. I'm no leader. I'm not worthy of Sarah either. The fog of memory swirls, and for a moment a memory is there, freezing me. No, that didn't happen. It doesn't matter.

Light breaks into the dark as they force the maw open. Ragnar takes my hand and pulls, helping me out of the creature.

Standing over the monster, we exchange looks, shaking our heads.

"Too close," I say.

"The wall took a lot of damage," Padraig says.

"We're going to need a way to keep them away from our area," Melchior says.

"Any bright ideas?" I ask, looking at each of the males in turn.

As I expect, none of them have anything to offer. Padraig shrugs, shaking his head.

"Maybe something that causes a vibration off out there," he says, pointing across the rolling sand dunes.

"Such as?" I ask, pushing down my anger.

"I don't know," he says

"Right," I say. "Carve this damn thing up. It will give us food for a long while."

The suns are barely above the horizon now. I should be well on my way, but I'm stuck here. The others set about butchering the zemlja, and I have to help them. I don't want them to know I've been going to see Sarah. If one of them mentions it to Visidion, it will cause trouble. I'm not ready to handle him yet. By the time we're finished, it's beyond full dark. After we haul the last of the meat into the compound, the work of preparing it for storage begins.

Once the Tribe sets to work on this, it's easy to slip away. No one expects me to do this work, so I won't be missed. Under cover of darkness, I dart beyond the wall and race across the dunes. Even running full speed, the meeting place is hours away. I only hope she'll be there when I arrive.

The moon hangs low in the sky tonight. The wispy clouds that drift across its face cast long shadows over the land. Tajss is beautiful at night. The sand, now rendered in shades of black and white, creates soft patterns with its striations. Letting my mind drift, the distance flies by without incident until at last I see the rock ahead. Catching a second wind, inspiration from being so close to her, I pour on the speed.

When I get to our rock, there is no sign of her. She's gone. Damn it. Damn it all!

Kicking the sand, a sudden rage grips me, and I punch the rock. The shock of pain cuts through my rage bringing me back to my senses. I missed her. Damn you, Visidion, for putting me through this. You should make your female change her mind!

Looking around, empty anger consuming my thoughts,

the pattern of rocks laid out on the sand catches my attention. A circle—that can't be natural.

I kneel and lean in close to see it better, and just then a cloud clears the moon and soft light illuminates the heart drawn in the circle. My own heart skips a beat seeing it. She left this for me. I know it, it has to be her.

Sighing I rise. She was here, so she's okay. At least I know that much.

They'll need food. Every time we meet, I kill something that she can later find to feed them. I can't do it often enough to keep them well fed but at least she's not starving. She'll come looking, so I better leave something.

Kicking the rocks until they look random again, I turn my attention to finding a bivo. I'll leave it close to here. If I stay with it until shortly before sunrise, it should be safe from other predators. Looking across the distance, I can see the dim outline of the humans' ship rising into the sky. Sarah is there. An urge to rush in and take her grips me suddenly. Unexpected, it's so strong I'm walking forward before I think.

I can't. She wouldn't come if I did.

She and I owe everything to Visidion and Rosalind. We can't betray them no matter how much I wish we could. Sighing, I turn away to hunt down a bivo for her to find.

5

SARAH

"*D*on't do this," Drosdan implores.

"I have to," I say, tears streaming down my face.

"You are my treasure," he says, as his strong hands grip my shoulders and pull me into him.

My breasts smash against his chest, my nipples harden to points, and wetness forms between my legs as his bulging erection digs into my stomach. It's so big, straining against the cloth of his pants.

"Yes," I exhale.

"Mine," he says, hands grabbing my ass, squeezing.

"Yours," I breathe.

He lifts me off my feet, pulling me up to meet his lips. My clit throbs, tight, needful. His tongue drives into my mouth claiming it as his. I open my mouth to welcome his advance, moaning into his kiss.

Turning, he presses me against the wall, bulging muscles crushing me in just the right way....

"Sarah, wake up!"

The dream shatters. As soon as I blink my eyes open,

bright light assaults them. Covering my eyes with my hands, smacking my lips, I wave away whoever is hovering over me.

"Go away," I mutter, my throat so dry and parched that it comes out as a croak.

"No way," Tessa says.

Rolling over and throwing an arm over my eyes, I ignore her. She grabs my shoulder and pulls me back towards her.

"No," I grouse. "Let me sleep."

"You've already slept half the day," she says.

"But it was a good dream," I sigh, slamming my hands against the floor.

"Any dream is better than here," she agrees. "But we have to get moving. You're supposed to lead a patrol for food."

I finally open my eyes, groan, and sit up.

"Damn it," I bitch.

"I know," Tessa says, shrugging.

"What time is it?" I ask, wiping sleep from my eyes.

"Suns have been up for at least four or five hours," she says. "You're sleeping the day away!"

I stretch and yawn. As far as she's concerned I've slept for a lot of hours, but she doesn't know I was out until sunrise.

"Fine," I say, rising to my feet. "Is there anything left for breakfast at least?"

Tessa's face falls and it's all the answer I need. Another day of tightening the belt. Hopefully Drosdan made it and left something for me to find. If not, we're going to be going hungry again.

"They cut the rations again," Tessa says.

Nodding I exhale hard then square my shoulders.

"It's okay," I say. "Maybe we'll have good luck today. Then we'll eat like Queens tonight."

"Yeah," Tessa smiles.

My clit throbs, the empty ache in my core begging to be filled as the last vestiges of my dream cling to my thoughts.

It's distracting to have such thoughts overriding the basic need to survive. It's not like I've slept with Drosdan, so how can I be missing something I haven't had? There's never been time in my life for a lover. On the ship I was just coming of age, and since we've been here my work with Rosalind has taken up all my time.

Besides, no man ever caught my attention, not in that way anyway. Stomachs grumbling, Tessa and I make our way out of the quarters we share with the other three girls. I need something to get my mind off of that dream. I can't get it out of my head. He felt so good pressing against me, holding me against that wall, his tongue driving into my mouth and his cock digging into my stomach.

Is his cock really as big as I dreamed? I know the rumors about the Zmaj cocks, but are they true? If they are, can it fit in me? I know other girls have, obviously, but we're not all made the same. What if he hurts me? What if it feels too good?

Stop! Good god, Sarah, get a grip.

"So, Jackson," I say, trying to divert my attention.

Tessa looks over, her face flushing bright red. Then she quickly hangs her head, covering her face with her hair.

"He's fine," she says, not looking.

"That much is obvious," I tease.

"Oh!" she exclaims, shaking her head, and I laugh.

"So did you?" I ask.

"Did I?" she asks, then suddenly she looks at me, eyes wide and mouth hanging open.

"Yeah, did you?" I grin.

"He... I... we... uh..." she sputters, unable to get a word out.

"Uh-huh?" I encourage, not letting her off the hook.

"It's... I... well... you know, he's... nice," she says, shaking her head.

40

"Nice?" I ask.

"Yes," she says, nodding, confidence growing.

"How nice?" I ask, arching an eyebrow, taking a perverse pleasure in putting her through the wringer.

Anything is better than the tight ache in my core that keeps pulling at my attention.

"Nice, you know," she shrugs.

"Is he nice... down there?" I ask.

"Oh god, Sarah!" she exclaims, and I laugh letting her off the hook at last.

"I'm teasing," she says. "I'm glad you two are getting along. It must be nice to have someone," I say.

"Do you have anyone?"

"No," I lie. "No one for me."

"I could to talk to Jackson, I'm sure he'd help," she offers.

"No!" I exclaim too quickly, and the consequences for my vehemence are the surprise and confusion on her face.

"I was just offering," she says, hurt.

"I'm sorry, it's... fine. I'm not interested, you know? I've got a lot on my plate right now."

"I get that," she says. "We'd all be a lot worse off without you."

"Thanks," I say, my core pulsing its need again. "I need to do something before we head out, could you go tell the others I'll be along pretty quick. Maybe they can clean the guns before we go out?"

"Sure," she says, smiling.

I can't get him out of my head. Is he okay? Of course he's okay. Then why wasn't he there last night?

Something delayed him, that's all. He's fine. So, so damn fine. Big, strong, muscles bulging in so many places. The dream creeps out of the recesses of my thoughts, consuming them. My face is flushing warm again as I feel him pressing against me, holding me tight, his strong hands working my ass.

I've got to have relief. I can't go out hunting this distracted.

I glance up and down the hall—I'm alone. An idea pops up, and I make my way quickly through the ship, over the bulkhead, and into the old showers. The ship is mostly on its side, so I have to lower myself down onto a sink, and then climb down to what is now the floor. I stop and listen.

"Anyone in here?" I ask.

My voice echoes off the metal and porcelain of the shower room slash bathroom. I don't want to be caught, so I go to the nearest stall and shut the door behind me, just in case someone does come exploring.

The latch clicks, metal on metal, then I slide down to sit on the floor. I let the memory of the dream swim up to the surface of my mind. Spreading my legs wide, sliding my hand into my pants, fingers seeking my core. Wetness guides me in. When those fingers pass over my clit, a shudder runs through me as pleasure explodes, causing muscles to spasm and clench tight.

Biting my lip to hold back my moan, I let my fingers become his.

Pressing hard, circling, he works my clit, preparing me. He kisses his way along my shoulder, my neck, across my cheek to my lips. His tongue drives into my mouth as his hand presses hard against me, moving faster.

I can't hold back a groan, he feels so good. Wetness forms on my delicate lips, inviting more.

Sliding a finger in, probing deep, it's nowhere near the size of him. His hot kisses claim my lips over and over as his hand works faster. I grab my breasts with my free hand and tease them through my shirt. The fabric moves across the hard nipples making my thoughts explode.

Sliding a second finger inside myself, soft walls expanding to accommodate, closer to what I imagine his hand would be.

I let my breast go, finding my clit with that hand and rubbing it. Hard, fast circles as I drive the fingers of my other hand in and out. My wetness easily takes my two fingers, but I know he's so much bigger than this still. Can I take him?

The way his cock dug into my stomach in my dream, being crushed between us—it was huge. All the girls have talked about how big the Zmaj are, and not just big either. In hushed whispers, especially here in this camp, they talk about the ribs. How good it would feel to have those hard ridges sliding into you. That's what the experienced girls say, but what do I know of it?

Bigger. He's going to be bigger, and I want him. Want him to fill me with his massive, huge cock, driving deep inside me just like my fingers are, seeking out my core. Filling the pounding need inside me. This time when I pull my fingers out of my slick tunnel, I add a third before shoving them in again. Deep inside myself, I spread my fingers out, forcing my body to adjust to something bigger than it's ever had in it before.

That sensation rips its way through me, my muscles contract, my back arches, and I'm moaning through my clenched teeth, unable to hold back. Pressing hard against my clit as the spasms cause shuddering responses until, at last, the pleasure passes. Collapsing backwards, breathless, panting as my heart pounds in my chest. Slowly I catch my breath and the flush on my skin cools. I stand up and straighten my clothes before exiting the stall.

I've kept them waiting long enough. I have to hurry.

What used to be hangar bay is now the main living area of the Gershom's camp. It's the point where the ship opens onto the world outside. Stacked crates form a wall between inside and out, but the double red suns shine bright in this area, and sand forms most of the floor. People are all over this area, some of them working, some lounging around. Unfortunately, there's not a lot to do, a weakness of Gershom's. Rosalind understands that if you keep people busy, they are happier. It gives them something to think about besides how bad their situation is.

It's a key difference between him and her. I've done what I can to encourage people to be active and busy, but I'm not the leader. There's been little to no progress in making the ship into a home. Little to no progress in increasing the odds of our survival either. Tessa, Jackson, and Brian, another guy who fancies himself a hunter, are waiting by the opening in the crates that leads outside. Plastic tarps cover the opening, rattling in the hot breeze that almost always seems to be blowing across the dunes of Tajss.

"About time," Jackson says as I approach.

"Right," I say, carefully not thinking about my side trip. "Ready to go?"

"We've been ready," Brian says, motioning between the three of them.

"Okay," I say, ignoring the implied questions. "Let's roll out."

Grumbling, they pick up the packs at their feet and I grab mine. Taking weapons from a nearby table, we emerge onto the white striations of the sand dune. Rolling sand stretches before us all the way to the horizon. Color variations, shades of red to white, make it beautiful to look at. If only it didn't suck so bad living in this interminable heat. Holding hope that Drosdan did make it last night, I set off in the direction of our meeting place.

"Why are we going this way again?" Brian asks. "We should set out the other direction."

"Why?" I ask. "We've had good luck going this way, why break the pattern?"

"Because how many times can we luck onto a dead bivo in the same direction?" he asks, sarcasm dripping from every word.

Staring at him I wonder if he suspects the truth. No, how could he? I've been really careful about this.

"Look, it's what works. You want to lead your own group, you go do that. Got it?" I ask, hands on hips leaning towards him aggressively.

Thank you Rosalind. Rosalind says when someone is onto your plan, attack, don't retreat. It makes you look guilty if you back off.

"Fine," Brian huffs, stepping back. "We'll go your way, again."

"Good," I snap.

Tessa and Jackson look between the two of us, carefully not getting involved. Pushing past them, I head across the desert. The double red suns beat down. The heat is oppressive and the sand pulls down, sucking us in. Traveling on Tajss, if you're human, sucks. The Zmaj are built for this place—we're not. Lana built some shoes for getting across the desert, but everything went to shit back in the City before anyone could make enough to hand around. Thanks, Gershom, dick.

My head hurts, not bad, but a constant throbbing. My lips are chapped, mouth dry, and throat scratchy. I'm past due for epis, but not far enough to suffer withdrawal yet. Keeping myself in epis is the trickiest part of being a plant in Gershom's camp. I can't be seen taking it. That's a sure give-away that I'm a Zmaj sympathizer. Not seeing Drosdan last night has left me with a low level of anger. It pulses inside me, dancing at the edge of my thoughts, threatening to explode at the slightest provocation.

It's ridiculous, but behind it there is fear. What if something happened to him? Is he okay? I can't imagine he would miss our meeting for anything. The fact that he did means something happened. What? It's nothing, he's fine. He has to be fine. Has to be. What would I do if he isn't? No, don't go there. I'm not going to entertain that as a thought. He's fine. He has his responsibility to the Tribe as much as I do to Rosalind. They don't know he's coming to see me anymore than I've let Rosalind know. It's our secret. Some things she doesn't need to know.

If he's okay. He has to be. Damn it, my thoughts are circling. You better be okay, Drosdan, damn it.

Tessa and Jackson are giggling as they help each other across the sand. Brian is sulking, keeping himself off to one side, which is fine with me. I don't want to hear him grumping anyway. Stopping for water and watching Tessa and Jackson, a pain shoots deep into my chest. It takes me a moment to recognize it, but I envy them. They're making eyes at each other, laughing, and just happy.

Being envious is stupid. I'm happy for them in truth, but it does make me miss Drosdan even more. Not that any of these three would understand that. How could I be interested in an alien? He's not like us, he's different, he has scales, wings, and oh god, he has a tail. Blah, blah, blah. He's also kind, with a fierce loyalty that I can't help but admire. His persistence is admirable. So many qualities about him that are... perfect. He's what I've always wanted, everything I dreamed of in a man when I was a little girl.

So what if he has scales and horns? I think they're sexy.

"We should get moving," Brian grouses.

"Right," I agree.

The suns rise to midday by the time we get close to the rock. My heart is pounding in my chest. If there's no meat here, it's worse than no food, which is bad enough, it means that something is really wrong. It would mean he didn't make it at all. I keep biting my dry, chapped lip as the distance to the rock closes. It will be there. Drosdan is fine. Nothing happened.

Please, please be there.

"Are you okay?" Tessa asks, startling me.

Trying to compose my face, I look quickly away then realize that alone makes me look guilty of something. Damn it.

"Yes, why?" I ask, turning back and meeting her gaze.

Face it head on, I hear Rosalind say in my mind.

"Nothing, I guess, you just seem… distracted," she says.

Closing my eyes, I take a deep breath then let it out slowly.

"Right," I say, Tessa puts a hand on my shoulder, dipping her head down so she's looking into my eyes despite her being taller. "It's nothing. I'm tired, hungry, dehydrated, and…"

She leans in closer, expectant as I trail off talking. And what? What do I say to her? I glance around. Brian and Jackson are a short distance away and apparently not paying attention.

"What is it?" she prompts.

"I'm worried," I admit, the truth if only part of it.

"Aren't we all?" she asks.

"Yeah," I agree, hoping she'll leave it at that, but I'm not so lucky, she leans in closer, confidential.

"What worries you the most?" she asks.

My stomach knots into a hard ball and bile rises in my throat. I'm on thin ice. Mind racing, sifting through possible answers. What do I say?

"The future," I blurt out.

"Me too," she says, gripping my shoulder tight. "We can't stay at the ship. We won't make it."

"Right," I agree, too quick maybe, but latching onto the lifeline she's throwing me. "We need water and a food supply."

"Exactly!" she says, voice rising.

The two men look over at us before resuming their own conversation. The hair on back of my neck is standing on end, catching the beads of sweat dripping.

"Shhh," I admonish, glancing over at them.

"Oh, Jackson knows," she assures me.

"Brian?"

Her mouth opens, about to speak, when she glances over at him, and it snaps shut. Pursing her lips, she nods.

"Sorry," she says, shaking her head.

"It's fine," I say. "I don't want any trouble. You know how these things go."

Frowning, she grips my shoulder then releases. Giving her a tight smile, I turn and start walking, trusting the others to fall in with me. Or not. I'm not sure I care. All I can think about is Drosdan. Focusing all my attention on one foot in front of the other helps. No room for other thoughts. That tightness in my stomach? Nothing, only that next step. Pulling my foot out of the sand, placing it down, sinking in, and repeating with the other foot.

Head down, focus, step, step, step. Muscles aching, thighs trembling, it overrides the sick feeling. Jackson curses from behind me but I ignore it. There is going to be food waiting for us. Something lying dead, waiting. There is going to be because that means Drosdan is okay. Everything else will work out fine. He's okay, he was late, no big deal.

The shadow of the rock outcropping falls across me, easing the suns' stabbing rays in my eyes. Looking up and blinking away sweat to clear my vision, I see it. A bivo lying on its side, throat ripped out as if some monster killed it, then left it. Cool relief rushes through me, and I shudder with the force of it. Tears well unbidden in my eyes. Wiping them away furiously I stumble forward.

"Son of a bitch," Brian exclaims.

"Yay!" Jackson shouts. "We get to eat. That will be at least a week of food."

I walk over to the carcass and rest my hand on it. It's warm from the double suns beating on it. Fly-like insects buzz up from it, making a dark cloud in the air, some of them nibbling at me to see if I'm edible, too. I don't care. He's okay. Taking a deep breath, I brace myself, getting my emotions under control before I face the others. Exhaling slowly, pushing out the relief and the fear, I turn.

"We have work to do," I order.

"How can this be?" Brian asks, eyes narrowing, mouth forming a hard line of suspicion.

"Does it matter?" Tessa asks. "Seriously? You want to look a gift in the mouth? Are you stupid?"

"There's no way that we can keep finding food in the same area. Are you all crazy? This can't be a coincidence," he argues.

"And what, you'd rather be hungry?" Jackson asks, pulling his pack off his back.

"No," Brian grouses, glaring at me. "But it's not right. Something is off."

"What do you want me to say?" I ask. Attack, always attack, Rosalind whispers in my head. "I don't know how or why, but I'm thankful. You have some better idea? Or do you have some grand conspiracy you'd like to share with the rest of us?"

"Maybe," he says, doubt in his voice.

"Oh, yeah?" I ask, stepping towards him, leaning in to his space. "Tell us about it. What? You think maybe I have some secret pact with... what? Who?"

"Well, it could be," he says, unconsciously stepping back.

"Oh? With who? Or is it a what?" I press.

"I don't know," he says. "It's doesn't make sense, that's what I'm saying. How many times have we found something like this in the same area? What are the odds?"

"Who cares?!" Jackson interjects. "I'm hungry. Let's butcher this thing and get home. It sucks out here."

"Right?" Tessa agrees.

Brian and I glare at each other, neither of us willing to break our gaze but I see the doubt in his eyes. His mouth turns down, his hand trembles, then his eyes dart towards Jackson. I've got him.

"If you have something to add, do it," I say through gritted teeth. "Accuse me of whatever the hell it is you're thinking."

His eyes dart back to me widening.

"I..."

"You what?" I ask, stepping closer.

He's bigger than me by at least six inches and has probably close to a hundred pounds on me but he's wavering. Rosalind always said size doesn't matter in the face of confidence. Hold your position and don't back down. He wavers, not meeting my eyes. The tension between us builds until his shoulders slump, and he shakes his head.

"Nothing," he says. "Let's get this done."

I don't say anything. I watch him slide the pack off his back and move towards the carcass. The three of them set to work harvesting the meat and preparing it for the journey home.

"I'm going to the bathroom," I call out, making my way towards the protruding rock and walking around it for a semblance of privacy.

Tessa looks over and smiles, then returns to working. On the far side of the rock, I go to the spot where I left the sign for Drosdan. I know he was here, there's no way a bivo decided to randomly die right there. My heart rate increases on spotting the scattered stones I left in a circle. The heart I drew in the sand inside is still there, but now there's an arrow piercing through it. Our secret sign. A smile spreads across my face to the point it hurts. Kicking at the sand I cover over the sign. Happiness expands in me until I feel like I'm walking on air. Turning a circle, something in the rock itself catches my eye. A glint flashes as my gaze passes over it.

Inside a crevasse is a glass vial. When I work it free I'm holding a small bottle inside of which is a piece of paper. My stomach sinks. Rosalind. Does she know Drosdan has been helping?

Working the paper out of the glass I glance around for prying eyes before unrolling it.

Received. Good work.

She got my last report. Heaviness falls on my shoulders as the enormity of my task is thrust forward. It's all on me, survival of this group, and making sure Rosalind is aware of Gershom's plans. No pressure, Sarah. The fate of humanity and the surviving Zmaj, that's all. No big deal. You got this.

I crumple the paper in my fist, pop it in my mouth, and swallow it. After checking for watchers again, I put my own piece of paper back in the vial and replace it in the crevasse, then go to help with the butchering.

6

DROSDAN

"Visidion wants you to come to the City," Samil repeats.

"Why?" I snarl.

Samil shrinks away, ducking and shaking his head.

"I don't know," he whines, holding his hands up.

"If you're lying to me," I say, letting the threat hang.

"I'm not!" he exclaims.

This is bad. If Visidion wants me in the City, that means something is up. I'm supposed to be here, running the Tribe. My hands are automatically balling into fists, and I'm itching to hit something. Samil cowers before me, whimpering.

"Bah!" I exclaim, dropping my fists and shaking my head in frustration. "Fine. Ragnar!"

Ragnar walks over with a slow saunter. Olivia comes with him, a smile on her face, her hair fluttering in the warm breeze. Her face blurs in my vision, and I'm looking at Sarah. They don't look anything alike but my chest aches. Emptiness swells from deep inside, and my hearts skip a beat. Red rage roars, burning thought away. Clenching my fist, closing my eyes, struggling to remain in control.

"What's going on?" Ragnar asks.

Opening my eyes, his arm around Olivia holding her close, I see her now as her. The ache pounding in my chest doesn't ease, but the anger recedes.

"I have to go to the City," I say.

"Why?" Olivia asks.

"Visidion wants me there," I say.

"Sure. You need anything?" Ragnar asks.

"No," I respond. "Watch over things here. I'm leaving now."

"I'll handle things," he says.

"Keep an eye on Padraig and see if we can get Errol some help repairing the damage to the wall."

"Melchior and Bashir will help," he says.

Olivia's hand rests on his chest, her head leaning against him. Pain stabs into my chest so I turn away.

"I'll be back," I say, throat tight.

I walk away before I do something I'll regret. An itch forms between my wings where I can feel their eyes boring into me. Rolling my shoulders, I try to ignore the feeling.

Errol is hammering on a stone, trying to knock it back into line with the rest of the wall. Even though he's swinging the hammer as hard as he can, it's ineffective. As his arm swings again, I reach out and grab the hammer before it makes contact. His head snaps toward me, mouth turning down.

"What the-" he stops, seeing me, then lets the hammer go.

Looking the stone over, I turn sideways, positioning the hammer. Swinging with all I've got, pouring all my frustration and anger into the blow, I take aim and the hammer makes contact with the stone. It slams into alignment with the rest of the wall.

"Damn..." Errol hisses.

The humans' swear words have worked their way into

our language. Errol stares at me, mouth agape, shaking his head. I hold the hammer out to him and he takes it without a word. Feeling slightly better, I pass through the opening in the wall and head across the desert towards the City.

❦

THE DOME GLITTERS AS I COME CLOSER. I'LL BE THERE SOON and then I'll see. The suns set low on the horizon, their final rays bouncing off the City's dome, making rainbows of color shoot across the dunes. Feet pounding on the sand with each leap, accenting my thoughts with each impact. Anger pulses with each beat of my hearts. There's only one reason Visidion would call me to the City. It can't be that, but it has to be.

If he orders me to stop helping Sarah…

No, he can't do that. I won't. I can't.

Can I defy him?

Technically I have been, but he never said not to help her. I know he believed it was understood. I should have killed Gershom. If Sarah hadn't stopped me, none of this would be happening. The simplest answer was—and is—to take out Gershom.

Damn it, that's another circle. I can't change the past, no matter how much I want to.

The past. The swirling fog of my memories swells and recedes, throwing bits and pieces of flotsam out of the unknowing blankness from before the devastation. Things I don't want to remember. Images that can't be, that wasn't me. It can't have been me.

Pictures of bodies spread around me, blood-splattered hands held up before my face. It can't be real, nothing like that happened.

Maybe Visidion wants something else. A new plan or an

in-person report on the progress of the gardening. That could be all this is. Or the epis. In the last report I sent to him, I made it clear the epis supply is not going to last much longer. That's a definite concern—the humans aren't going to survive without it. We might be able to get red-leaved lychnara for them to break the addiction, but it wouldn't help them survive the heat. Their bodies aren't made for Tajss.

That has to be what this is. It's about the epis.

Yes, epis. What will we do about epis?

Cresting the final dune before the City, I pause. Staring at the dome causes the fog of the past to stir. Dim memories rise and fall. Before, Tajss was a different place. I was different then. Wasn't I?

Bursting into a run, I sprint, closing the distance between the City and me. The memories try to chase me, but I have no use for them. This, right now, this moment is all that matters. What came before is done. All that matters is what I do now. A deep, niggling thought, that if I run fast enough I'll outrun the memories, that thought rises, but I push it aside too. There is nothing to run from because it's nothing.

When I reach the airlock, I punch in the code and wait for the door to cycle open. A whoosh of air flushes out as it opens, and I step inside. When I enter the next code, the door behind me closes, air pours in from vents above, and then the inner door opens. The City lies before me.

Stepping onto the processed stone of the street is strange. It doesn't give to my weight like the sand outside. Empty streets ache with loneliness and what was. Decay weighs heavy on the buildings. Broken windows. Twisted steel. The aftermath of the Devastation. Shaking myself free of the sense of melancholy the City evokes in me, I jog ahead, passing by empty buildings as I make my way to the City center.

As I get closer to the center, I see humans going about

their day, male and female. They wave or smile as we pass one another, and I nod to them without slowing my pace. I want to get this over with. It isn't long enough before I'm walking past the main fountain, where lots of people are gathered, visiting and collecting water. I enter the main building and work my way up to Rosalind's offices and the Council meeting space.

"Drosdan," Ladon says, as I step out of the stairwell.

Ladon isn't as big as I am, but there's a confidence about him. He's a fighter, self-assured, and he's in his home. The City was his alone when the humans crashed here, and he still considers it to be his. Everyone else lives here by his will alone, at least in his mind. I'm not sure Rosalind would agree with that assessment, but she lets him believe it.

"Where are they?" I ask without preamble.

Ladon nods towards a double set of doors that lead into the council chambers. Squaring my shoulders, I walk to the doors and throw them open. Inside Rosalind and Visidion sit at the far end of the long table, deep in a discussion. The doors bang against the walls, and I squeeze my large frame into the opening. They look up, faces serious, but neither of them speak. I have met their gaze, and now I wait for them. The silence stretches to the point of becoming uncomfortable. My scales itch and my hands twitch. I hate waiting.

I sense more than hear Ladon behind me, but I continue waiting. It's a matter of dominance. I won't give first. Visidion and I lock eyes, and a contest of wills ensues. Rustling my wings, my tail still, I pour myself into the stare, willing him to give. The moment becomes a minute and stretches further. Neither of us willing to bend. The contest continues.

"All right, enough," Rosalind says, her words cutting, but neither of us breaks our gaze to look at her. "We're friends here, you two can stop the pissing contest."

Rosalind places a hand on Visidion's.

"Right," he says, clearing his throat. "Come on in, Drosdan."

I can't stop the smile that forms as I walk across the room and take a seat opposite Visidion. Ladon comes behind me and takes a seat next to me.

"I'm sure you're wondering why you're here," Rosalind says.

"Yes," I reply.

No need to say more, this is going to be what it's going to be.

"You've been helping Gershom," Rosalind says.

Visidion's hand clenches into a fist, anger boils off him in hot waves slamming against me. My tail shifts back and forth, and my stomach tightens into a hard ball. Eyes narrowing, I watch Visidion.

"If I have?" I ask.

"If you have, you've directly defied me!" Visidion barks.

"In what?" I ask.

"You know damn well I don't want you helping them," he says, leaning forward, elbows on the table between us.

"Do I?"

His mouth tightens and eyes narrow as he rises to his feet.

"You would dare defy me," he says, voice barely above a whisper.

An image flashes to the front of my mind. Another Zmaj leaning in, spittle flying from his mouth, eyes bloodshot, screaming at me to follow the order.

Cold shock races through my limbs, my heart skips a beat, and I'm left shaken. I blink rapidly to clear the image from my mind. Visidion is leaning across the table, angry, but it's not him in the memory.

"Visidion," Rosalind says in a calming voice.

"I will not be defied," he hisses, pulling his hand free of her touch.

"There is a better way to handle this," Ladon says.

"Do you defy me?" Visidion asks.

The same image rises, confusing the situation. Almost I remember, and it's pulling at me. Sickness bubbles in my stomach. No, I can't do this. I can't follow the order. It's wrong.

"I…" I say, but words fall apart.

Sarah's voice, soft and beautiful, *'I have to,'* she whispers.

Have to, have to, no choice. Follow orders, obey, it's what we do. Her and I, we obey those above us. We follow orders.

"You what?" Visidion asks. "Have you been helping them or not?"

Meeting his gaze full on, a cold resolve forms in my guts, and it brings calm.

"Yes," I say.

"I knew it," he growls. "You've betrayed me, Drosdan. You of all people, I never would have expected it."

"Drosdan, explain yourself," Rosalind says.

"Explain myself? You sent her out there, alone, with those animals!"

"You know why—"

"I know your excuses!" I yell, cutting her off. Visidion hisses, his tail rising. When I slam my fist on the table there's a snapping sound, and a crack appears in the thick wood. "I'm done."

"Drosdan," Ladon says, but holds his hands up when I turn towards him. "We can work this out."

"No, we can't," I say. "I shouldn't have let her go. It was stupid. She's mine, and I won't leave her out there, alone, any longer."

"Drosdan, they have to survive on their own," Rosalind says.

"Then let them, without her!" I yell.

Turning my back on them, I storm towards the door. My scales itch, expecting an attack, but nothing happens. When I jerk the door open it slams against the wall.

"Drosdan," Visidion says, his voice soft, cutting through the raging anger burning through my body.

I stop and wait for what he's going to say.

"There is a better way," Rosalind says. "Please, we can work this out."

"There's nothing to work out. I'm saving her," I say.

"We need more time," Visidion says. "I know how you feel, but give us time."

"I gave you time. I've given you everything. I won't leave her there—it's done," I say.

Ladon says something, but I don't hear his words. The stairwell door closes behind me, cutting them off. I'm coming, Sarah. Ready or not, we're done with them. I'm going to save you.

7

SARAH

"*H*OLY SHIT! THEY'RE COMING!"

Hot wind flutters the plastic sheeting covering the opening in the generation ship. Everyone working inside the open area looks up. A cold chill runs down my spine from more than sweat. Dozens of us exchange glances, some shaking their heads, a few going back to sorting through supplies, pretending they didn't hear a thing.

Someone runs in, bursting through the plastic, arms waving wildly in the air. My eyes don't adjust fast enough to make out who it is. All I see is a shadowy figure who looks like he's bouncing up and down.

"They're coming," he screams. "Get the weapons! We have to hide, we have to run!"

Blinking rapidly, trying to force my eyes to adjust, I run over to the shadow shape.

"Who's coming?" I ask.

A few others come with me including three armed men. Gershom only trusts a few people with weapons, even in his own group. He doesn't say that, of course, bad PR if he did, but I see what he's doing more than anyone else here is willing to.

"The Zmaj! There's an army of them, running right for us! This is it!"

The three armed men push past the one screaming and step around the plastic. Andrew, the one who's screaming, glances at them as they go, then turns back to the crowd gathering around him.

"Calm down," I say.

"It's just like he said," Andrew says. "Gershom told us this would happen. They only wanted to get us out of sight so no one would know what they do to us!"

The crowd murmurs in agreement. Fear races between them in palpable waves. This is ridiculous and I know it. It's also dangerous. I don't know what is happening, but I know damn well it's not some genocidal slaughter ordered by Rosalind or any of the Zmaj. A woman next to me bursts into tears, shuddering as her body is wracked by sobs. All of them are pale, scared, and becoming a mob.

"That's ridiculous," I say, raising my voice to be heard by everyone. "The Zmaj aren't going to come kill us all."

"They're going to kill us!" someone cries out.

"That's not what I said!" I yell.

"She said it, Gershom is right, they're coming to kill us. We have to fight," someone says.

"I'm not going out without a fight!" a man shouts.

Cold chills form bumps on my arms. This is getting out of hand fast. I'm jostled by the growing crowd, stumbling into the crate in front of me.

"Wait!" I shout, but so is everyone else, and my voice is drowned in the cacophony of fear. As the noise grows, so do their emotions, hitting against me in waves, making my heart race. I climb up onto the crate I was shoved into, and then I turn and face them, cupping my hands around my mouth. "LISTEN!"

I scream at the top of my lungs to be heard. Silence falls like a heavy blanket. Dozens of people stare at me, wide-eyed, shaking in place. Looking for answers.

"Don't be scared," I say.

"What in the hell does that mean?" a man shouts.

"Look, they're not going to kill us. Go and hide, and I'll go out and deal with whatever is happening."

"Who made you leader?" a woman asks.

"Where's Gershom?" someone else asks.

"Do we really have time for this? They're right out there," I point behind me. "You want to sit here debating or get to safety?"

They look at each other, muttering, then the people in the back head off into the ship. After the first ones go, the rest follow. Taking a deep breath, I hold it until the last of the crowd disperses. I let it out and jump down, then head out to see what is what. The double red suns blind me again as I step onto the soft sand. Shielding my eyes, I look out across the desert expecting to see an army of people heading for us. Ahead of me, kneeling with weapons ready, are the three armed men crouching behind the artificial wall made of crates. Following the line of their gaze I spot it.

One person.

Seriously? A person is coming, and we almost have a riot?

Still, one person is approaching. Which is weird enough, but it's also obviously a Zmaj. When I walk up behind the armed men, one of them jumps and swings his gun towards me.

"Whoa!" I shout, ducking to avoid being in the gun's line of fire.

"Shit, sorry," he says, turning back and setting his sights on the approaching figure.

Anxiety pulses along my nerves, the hair on my arms standing on end as sweat rolls. The mild headache beats too but I'm so used to it now that I barely notice it.

"What's going on?" I ask.

"No clue, but we're going to take it out," one of the men says, making a snickting sound as he sucks on his teeth.

"How about talking first?" I ask.

"Talking, schmocking," another answers. "I'm going to shoot the hell out of that monster."

Bile rises in my throat. The casual violence leaves me cold despite the heat. I don't know how anyone can be so... what? Mean? Angry?

Evil.

It's just evil. No better than the space pirates that caused our ship to wreck here in the first place. Though, despite all the bad things, I don't regret being here. If I wasn't here I'd never have met Drosdan, after all. I stare out across the sand. The distant figure with spread wings crests a dune and comes back in sight. Shielding my eyes again, I try to see who it is. It has to be someone I know. After all, there are only so many Zmaj. One of the men shifts his position, leaning in, his gun clicking.

"Don't shoot him!" I shout.

"Bang," he says, laughing.

I kick his leg as hard as I can, and he grunts, in surprise or pain, I'm not sure.

"I said, don't!" I yell.

"You aren't our boss," he growls. "Our job is to defend this outpost, for humans. That ain't no human out there."

"Let me talk to him," I say, hands on hips, staring down into his cold, hard eyes.

"No," he says.

"You're not a monster, and he hasn't done anything wrong," I counter.

Something moves in his eyes, he darts them to the side, then back to me.

"No," he says, shaking his head. "We've got to do this."

"No, you don't. Don't be an idiot. He's coming alone, what could possibly go wrong? I'll go out and talk to him. If he tries anything violent, then you can shoot him."

"You'll be in the way," one of the men observes.

"Then shoot me too," I say, exasperated.

The three of them look at each other, obviously unsure what to do with that. I don't wait for them to figure it out before walking past them and heading across the desert myself.

"Hey, you can't... we can't... Stay back here!" one of them shouts after me.

I give him a universal message with one hand and a finger over my shoulder without looking back. I hear them gasp then mutter to each other, but I don't care. I'm tired of their bull. They're part of Gershom's "special" team, the hand-picked ones he lets have weapons and the best of what little we have. All of which means they are blind idiots who buy into his nonsense whole cloth.

An itch forms between my shoulder blades, and I wonder, for a moment, if they won't shoot me too. These guys are jerks of the first degree. Arrogant and filled with self-importance as they lord it over the rest of us who followed Gershom into the desert like some kind of perverse messiah. I, at least, only pay lip service to his rhetoric. The longer we're out here, the more the regular folk are realizing that this isn't a good idea. I'm not sure if that's what Rosalind expects but it's absolutely happening. I think, given enough time, that the majority will decide to go back to the City and make nice with the Zmaj.

In time, though, is the problem. Right now someone is coming, and I don't know why. This wasn't part of any plan I was made aware of, so what is going on? Can I keep them from being shot?

The men behind me are still muttering and talking to each other. Each shift they make is accompanied by the sound of metal on metal. Their guns moving, shifting, a reminder that at any moment I could be electrocuted by thousands of painful bolts. I guess I can be thankful they don't have projectile weapons. Being electrocuted is better than being pierced by a bullet, I suppose. My preference would be neither happens though.

The sand pulls me in more as I start climbing the closest dune. It's always looser on the inclines, making it twice as hard to go forward. Leaning in, I push my body past the pain and discomfort. The grains of sand sparkle brightly, casting tiny rainbows from the suns' glare. No matter how much it hurts, I have to push through.

Cresting the dune, finally, I shield my eyes. The distant shadowy figure is much closer now. Blocking the sun away and blinking several times, I finally see who it is.

"Oh shit," I gasp. "No, no, no."

It can't be. Squeezing my eyes shut tight, I count to five before opening them again and staring. It is. Something has happened. Nerves tingling as if a mild shock is running through me I burst into a run. He's coming. I don't know what's wrong, but there's no way he'd be here, running straight for the camp, if it wasn't bad. Has something happened to Rosalind? One of the babies? My stomach turns, the hair on my arms standing on end, the pain and aches fade away as adrenaline dumps into my body. Every sense is on fire, stretching out and alert to danger with no clear source to watch for it from.

Drosdan shifts his direction, bearing straight down on me. He leaps forward in bounds, wings catching the slight wind current and gliding him across the sand, closing the distance between us fast. My heart pounds in my chest watching, making me light-headed. He's coming, for me.

"Get ready!" I hear one of the men behind me.

"No!" I yell, turning. "I'll handle this."

They're taking aim with their guns. This is going to get ugly.

"Get out of the way!"

"No!" I yell, turning my back on them. Drosdan is really close now. "Drosdan, stop!"

He's close enough for me to see him frown and shake his head, pumping his arms and legs faster, if anything. Another leap, high into the sky, and his shadow falls across me from impossibly high up. His wings spread, flapping, pushing him further ahead. He descends from the heavens, a god coming for me.

He lands a few feet ahead, sand spraying up from the impact, running the moment his feet hit the ground. Bending down, arms wide, he sweeps me off my feet, cradling me against his chest. Turning away from the armed men, he runs.

"I've got you," he says.

My heart leaps into my throat, making it impossible to respond. Electricity burns through the air as the men fire. Shouting follows behind it, but I can't make out their words. Swallowing hard to clear the lump in my throat, I'm struggling to control my raging emotions.

"What are you doing?" I ask.

"Saving you," he says, staring ahead as he zigs and zags from one side to another.

Electrical bolts zing around us as he dodges.

"You can't... we can't...."

Glancing down, he smiles. The light in his eyes melts my heart, unshed tears well in my eyes.

"I can, we can," he says, chuckling.

"But, Rosalind… Visidion…"

"No," he shakes his head in the negative.

An electrical burst slams into the sand just ahead of us, sending specks of it into my eyes. Blinking hard, trying to free my eyes of the invader, the tears have nothing to do with my out-of-control emotions. No, seriously, it's totally the sand.

"Drosdan, we can't. I have to stay here—Rosalind needs me," I say, bouncing in his arms as he continues bounding across the sand.

The shouts and the electricity hitting around us fade away. There is only Drosdan and Sarah. He stares into my eyes and becomes my entire world.

"She doesn't need you as much as I do," he says.

Everything stops. My heart, the sound, motions all comes to a halt. His eyes keep boring into me, driving in his words.

"Okay," I say. Unable and unwilling to argue further, I wrap my arms around his neck and let him carry me away.

8

DROSDAN

*T*his is a stupid plan. Stupid, but I don't have a better one. I was so angry at Visidion and Rosalind that I acted without thinking about it further. Even the run from the City to the wreckage where Gershom and his followers are wasn't enough to make me let go of the anger.

"Where are we going?" she asks.

The red suns are barely above the horizon, shadows creeping across the desert. It's a good question, one I wish I had an answer for. The storm inside me continues to rage. I hold it at bay through sheer force of will, strengthened by her. I know I'm heading for something, but I don't know what or where, at least not logically. Something is driving me this direction.

"I don't know," I answer her, shifting her weight.

"Oh," she says, snuggling her head against my neck.

I could run forever like this. Sarah in my arms, safe—the two of us together. Still a stupid plan, but that doesn't change how good she feels.

"We'll need to find an oasis," I say.

"What about the one we've used before?" she asks.

"They'll be going there, sooner or later. We can't be there if they do," I say.

"Oh," she says, the disappointment in her voice a heavy weight falling on me.

"You understand, don't you?" I ask, a sudden desperation grasping me.

She doesn't speak. Minutes pass in silence, anticipation building inside me.

"Yes," she says, finally. "I do, but..."

The "but" hangs in the air, filled with dread. Whatever follows it is not going to be something I want to hear. She doesn't say any more, and again the silence drags out, broken only by the soft sound of my feet hitting the sand and the whisper of my spread wings using the wind to carry us forward. I wait, a sense of foreboding pounding me until at last I can't take it.

"But?" I prompt her.

"Duty," she says, the simple word that carries so much with it.

It opens the black hole of despair that comes with it. Brief images flash across my thoughts, breaking them up, bodies scattered in front of me, broken and mutilated. Screaming, tears, pain, the red rage buries them and I hiss.

"It's a two-way street," I growl. "They betrayed us."

Glancing down, I see her frown before she buries her face against me. She tightens her grip around my neck but doesn't say anything. My hearts pound in my chest, anger driving them, making my breathing short and ragged. My muscles tingle with the urge to hit something, anything, to let the raging storm inside out. She doesn't understand. How can she? I can't explain it, none of it makes sense, but I know I'm right.

She doesn't say more, and I can't put my thoughts into words, so we travel west, towards the setting primary sun.

The land changes as we travel, the rolling dunes flattening, rocky protrusions appearing less often. Dimly I remember this area but it's been a very long time since I traveled this far. Dusk deepens and my stomach grumbles so I slow down and come to a stop. I lower Sarah to her feet and slide my pack off my back. I didn't come unprepared, even though I was acting on impulse. I get out some tinder from my pack and prepare a small fire, using my throat glands to set it ablaze. Earlier today I wrapped some smoked meat in oilcloth—now it seems like years ago. I also packed the folding skewers Zmaj use for travel, and now I thread chunks of meat onto a skewer and hold it over the fire.

Sarah sits across from me, knees pulled up in front of her and arms wrapped around them. The silence is heavy with unspoken words and thoughts. The whirlwind inside that hasn't stopped since my showdown with Visidion continues to swirl and rage. A mix of images, emotions, and the ever-present fog of the bijass tinged with the rage it brings. She has to understand. Somehow I have to make her. After holding the meat over the fire until it's sizzling, I offer it to her first. Daintily she works a piece off the skewer, then blows on it before popping it in her mouth.

Her perfect, sweet mouth. An urge to kiss her consumes me, and I'm leaning towards her before I know it. Until she pulls back, eyes wide, mouth open.

"Drosdan," she says. Stabbing, sharp pain drives into my hearts, forcing them to stop beating if only for a moment. The maelstrom in my head stops, replaced with cold that runs through my limbs. Drawing back from her, I nod and sit down on the opposite side of the fire. "I'm sorry," she whispers.

Staring at her, I can't find the words to answer. I try but nothing will come out of my mouth. She shakes her head, then raises her hands and drops them. One heart beats then the other follows suit, and the world goes back into motion, although seemingly slower than normal. Placing a piece of meat in my mouth, I fill the silence by chewing. Swallowing my voice finally returns.

"It's fine," I lie.

It's anything but fine. I don't know what this means.

"No, it's not," she says. "It's just... what are we doing?"

"Leaving," I answer, honest and blunt. "We don't need them."

"They need us," she says.

"No!" I say harsher than I intend but anger flashes hot. "They don't. They think they do, they use us, tell us what to do, and we act without thought or concern. They don't care about us, so why should we care about them!"

"Drosdan, you know that's not true," she says.

"It is," I say. "I asked, no I begged them not to send you out with him. Did they listen? No. Then when they found out I was giving you some aid, they ordered me to stop. How would you survive without it? Those people can't feed themselves! You would starve!"

Frowning, she stares at me from across the small fire casting flickering shadows across her face, making it impossible for me to read. She has to understand.

"So that's what happened," she says.

"What?" I ask, confusion hitting. It's not the response I expected.

"I knew something bad had to happen. You would never have done this otherwise."

Her soft voice cuts through the storm inside, pushing it aside and speaking truth that I can't deny.

"Yes," I agree. "I couldn't..."

I can't finish the words. They wanted me to stop, but the risk to her would have been too great. I couldn't live with myself. Sarah nods then sighs loudly. She stands, circles the fire, and sits down beside me, snuggling against me. When I put my arm around her shoulders, she lays her head on my chest. Her warms hands on my scales bring me all the comfort I need in the world.

"I get it," she says. "But what do we do now?"

"I'll take care of us," I say. "It will be like before. Before the Tribe, before the City, before all of it. Then I was alone, but now we will have each other."

"Okay," she says.

Her agreement is everything. It's as if the universe turns, and everything that was wrong becomes right. Quiet comes inside me, all the noise, the anger, and the bijass stops. When I'm holding her close, nothing else enters my thoughts. Her breathing evens out a few minutes after she lays her head on my chest. Slowly the moon rises into the sky, casting its silver light across the open sand. The fire's crackle slows as it dies to nothing but a small pile of glowing embers. Contentment, something I haven't felt in so long it takes me a while to recognize it, fills me. I can feel her heart beating against me, her warm breath crossing my scales, the touch of her soft skin on my fingers as I draw small circles on her back.

Time passes but I don't notice it going. My world is in my arms, and the depth of satisfaction I feel right now is absolute. A light breeze stirs the sand, sending sparks flying out of the coals of our fire, and then a cloud passes over the moon, casting a shadow over us. Sarah stirs, then stretches and yawns.

"Mm, sorry," she says, raising her head.

"It's fine," I say. "You needed the rest."

"Are we okay here? Should we move on?"

"When you're ready, we'll continue," I say.

"What about you, don't you need some sleep? I can sit watch," she offers.

Smiling, I shake my head, appreciating her concern.

"It's not necessary," I say.

"You're sure?"

"Yes," I say.

She frowns but doesn't argue further. Rising to her feet she stretches again and yawns. Climbing to my feet as well I close up my pack while she works out kinks.

"We're really doing this?" she asks, hands on her hips.

"You have a better idea?" I ask.

She purses her lips, frowning, her brow furrowing.

"No," she says, shaking her head at last.

"Then we're doing this," I say. "You want me to carry you?"

"I can walk, for now," she says holding her hand out to me.

I take hers in mine and lead the way. The silence between us is more comfortable, if not as good as when she was sleeping on my chest, but at least I don't feel like I'm walking on quicksand. Continuing west, the land is completely flat now. The sand is no longer soft like the rolling dunes of home, but hard packed, making travel easier. Glancing behind us, our footsteps leave an obvious trail, but there's nothing I can do about it. There is a soft breeze that will eventually erase the traces of our passage, before anyone stumbles across them, I hope.

The stars shine more brightly as the sky clears, and the silvery moon makes our travel easy. It would be difficult for anything to attack us without warning, which is good. Something, deep in my guts, recognizes the area. A dim familiarity that I can't put my finger on. Grasping at the concepts of it, it slips away like a zmeya snake, never coming to fruition.

"So, do we have a plan yet?" Sarah asks, pausing to drink some water from her canteen.

"Yes," I say, only partially lying.

"Oh?" she asks, arching an eyebrow. Moonlight touches

her brow making her eyes sparkle. Her beauty takes my breath. "And it is?"

Shaking my head, I try to cover my inability to speak. Swallowing hard, I push the lump in my throat down, willing my hearts to slow their beat.

"There's something ahead," I say.

"Something?"

"Yes."

"You realize that's really vague, right?" she asks, her voice musical with the delight and joy she brings to everything.

"Yes," I smile.

"And you're going to leave it at that?"

She steps closer, fingertips touching my chest, tracing along the edges of my scales, trailing fire with their passage. Staring into her bright eyes once more, I can't form words. Thought shatters at her touch. Impulsively, I bend to her and kiss her. Touching her soft, plump lips makes a fire blaze in my core as my primary cock engorges. She gives to me, pressing her body, molding against me. I wrap my arms around her and lift her off her feet, then spin around, holding her tight. She moans into the kiss, moving her hips in a grinding motion against me.

My cock pounds with desire, wanting to be buried inside her warmth. Hands on her perfect, round ass, squeezing, I drive my tongue past her full lips, claiming her mouth as my cock wants to claim her lower lips. Her tongue meets mine, wrestling for control, not giving in but being my match. The perfect mate, my treasure. A warm glow races out through my limbs, engulfing me and I feel it overtaking her as well. More than desire, more than need, it's a claiming. Marking her as mine and me as hers. We belong together—it is fate— binding us one to another.

A sharp screech cuts through the kiss. Crouching and setting her down at the same time, I reach for the lochaber on my back, ready for an attack. A shadow passes over, blocking out the moonlight. Overhead a flock of sismis passes, screeching loudly. With an arm around Sarah's waist, I gently pull her underneath me, spreading my wings to break up our outline. The only real danger to us from the pack is that there are too many of them. Alone, I could fight the entire pack, but having to keep her safe while dealing with them is too dangerous. It's much better if I can avoid them.

They pass overhead and then circle back. Sarah is breathing in ragged gasps beneath me, and I feel her tremble. I want to reassure her, but don't dare risk making a sound. Their screech is louder, so they're flying lower as they circle. Tightening my grip on the lochaber, muscles tensing, I'm ready to leap to the attack. They circle away again. Next pass, I'll attack. Watching in my peripheral vision, holding my breath, ready to move, I wait. Another screech, distant now, but they might still circle back. Tense, waiting, seconds crawling past.

Sarah exhales heavily, drawing another trembling breath. Her entire body shakes beneath me. Anger pulses through me, building towards a blinding rage. Nothing should make her feel this way. I am her protector.

An even more distant screech. They're retreating. Remaining a few moments more to be sure, at last I rise, helping Sarah to her feet as well. She looks around wide-eyed, then throws her arms around my chest, crushing herself against me.

"It's okay," I say, softly, enclosing her in my arms.

She sobs, shaking.

"I know," she says, still shaking.

I hold her, silent, unsure what words to say until she calms.

9

SARAH

I can't believe we're doing this.

I've never, ever considered leaving. I owe Rosalind everything, but what am I supposed to do? Drosdan is insistent that we leave. I don't want to, well mostly I don't. Part of me does. When he talks about the two of us living together, no worries but for each other, it calls to some deep part of me. A part of me I've ignored all my life. When he looks at me, his smoldering eyes, massive muscles bulging, that imposing presence, and I know that beneath that hard exterior is a soft, loving man, I can't help myself. He makes me feel like a princess.

Me, a princess.

I never thought of myself like that, not even in my dreams. I'm not the one in the spotlight, I'm the best friend. If I were in a movie, I'm the supporting actress, never the star. That's who I am, and I've always been good with that. I never wanted to be the star of the show. Until Drosdan.

He changed everything. When we met, I thought he was hot, of course I did, look at him. So strong, massive muscles, a jaw line that any alpha male would kill to have. I'm a girl and alive, after all, so why wouldn't I notice that he was sexy as hell? It's not like I was going to act on that, I'm not that kind of girl. It's never been his looks to me, those are a bonus.

He came to me, that first time, with a tiny, wilted flower. So small looking in his enormous hand, and he held it out to me, silent, staring at me with pleading eyes. His hand trembled. It trembled! Staring at the flower then looking into his eyes, I fell into them and lost myself. All like some kind of freak accident, unplanned, unexpected, but it felt so right.

We shouldn't be together. We have no right to it. Our lives are dedicated to our leaders, him to Visidion and me to Rosalind, but that very dedication kept bringing us into each other's presence. Sighing, I shake my head. Cold chills form in my stomach, combating the ever-present heat of Tajss. Drosdan's hand rests on the small of my back as we walk, the weight of it somehow reassuring.

Our first kiss comes to mind. We'd been working together secretly, of course, since shortly after I'd started infiltrating Gershom's camp. Our first meetings had been mostly accidental crossings of our paths, but those accidents started happening more and more often until I was certain he was making them occur. This had gone on for a long time. I'd be leaving a meeting with Rosalind, sneaking out of the building to make sure none of Gershom's followers spotted me, and he'd be waiting in the stairwell, or just happen to be coming through a door as I was passing by.

I can't help smiling remembering how he'd just happen to be there, without fail.

We'd talked a lot about everything, sharing our thoughts and hopes with each other. Then the kiss. Unexpected, but definitely not unwelcome.

His cool lips finding mine, his strong arms encircling me.

I'd jerked back, at first, but quickly gave in to his attention. Everything changed in that moment.

Now, at the memory, desire roars to life inside my core. His touch on the small of my back is a warm presence from which tingling need surges through my body.

When I glance up at him next to me, my lips ache for his, but in this place there is nothing but open exposed sand. No matter the urge, I can't give myself to him in the open wilds like this. No, it has to be something special. This would never do. Pushing desire away, thoughts spinning with the force of the urging in my body, I grasp for anything to take my mind off it.

"I can't believe we're doing this," I say the first thought that comes to me. He frowns but doesn't say anything. "I mean, it's just… crazy."

"It could be," he says, still he doesn't look at me, marching determinedly ahead.

"And?" I prompt after a while when he doesn't expand on the thought.

Shaking his head he shrugs.

"I don't care," he says.

"Oh," I say, unsure how to respond.

It spins my head how he's acting. Something is off with him, but I don't know what. We continue in silence, again, while I can do nothing but hope. Surely he'll tell me. I know he does care—really, I'm certain of that. The change has to have been caused by something. There's a solemnity to him that is new. He's always been serious, sure, rough on the outside even. A real tough guy, to everyone but me.

I don't know how long I wait. There's no measurement of time when you're trotting across the desert, but eventually I can't wait any longer so I break the silence.

"Drosdan," I say.

"Yes?" he asks.

"Tell me what's going on," I say, stopping.

He comes to a stop, turning to face me, bright eyes glittering in the rising suns' light. The beams of light bounce off his scales, creating tiny rainbows in the air between us. He crosses his bulging arms over his massive chest. His wings open partway, casting a shadow across me. Matching his pose, I meet his gaze, unwavering, waiting for him to answer.

"Only what I said," he says.

"Right," I agree. "I got that, now tell me the truth. There's something happening that you haven't told me."

His eyes break from mine, staring out across the empty desert behind us. His jaw tightens as his hands ball into fists. He inhales deeply, holding it in, puffing out his chest.

"I don't know," he says, exhaling.

"You don't know what?" I prod further.

He starts to shake his head, but then comes to some kind of decision and meets my eyes. The pain in his look causes an answering, stabbing pain deep into my heart. My breath catches in my throat as I'm rocked back by the depths of it in him.

"I don't... know. Memories, images—they make no sense."

I'm drawn into him as if he's a whirlpool sucking me closer. I can't keep myself from him. Closing the small distance between us, placing my hand on his chest, I run my fingers across his pecs, back and forth until he uncrosses his arms and welcomes me in. When I lay my head against his chest, the sound of his hearts races like the beating of horses' hooves galloping down a track. His arms close around me, and I place my own arms around him, holding him as much as he's holding me. His fingers run through my hair, down my back, then up again.

Heat rises as the suns crest the horizon on their daily climb. Holding him until his hearts slow their pace to something closer to normal, the time passes and I don't care. Once

I hear them slow, I pull my head off his chest, but keep my arms wrapped tight around him.

"Talk to me," I say.

His jaw tightens, and for a moment I think he won't. It drags on, slow, then at last he speaks.

"It's hard to explain," he says.

"Okay," I reassure him.

"The bijass, it eats our memories, leaving in its wake bits and pieces."

"I'm familiar with it," I say.

Frowning he shakes his head.

"Except, maybe it doesn't. Maybe that is what we tell ourselves. It's a fog, in my mind, rising and falling, pushing forward then retreating. Bringing with it rage and primal desire, but when it retreats, sometimes, it leaves behind fragments. I can't follow them blindly, not any longer."

"It's okay," I say, tracing the line of his jaw with my fingers.

"No, it's not. It goes against every fiber of who I am, but I can't, not when it comes to you. You are... everything. I will not follow any order that leaves you in danger. No longer."

Tension enters his words, rising, as anger rushes over him.

"Okay, Drosdan, I understand," I say, trying to be reassuring.

"No, you don't," he says, voice harsh, taking a step back. "I won't let them come between us. I won't let anything happen to you. You're my treasure, and if they can't see that, then they can go back to space and not return. We don't need them—we've given enough."

He makes slashing motions with his hands as he speaks, growing more agitated with each word.

"Drosdan, please," I say, trying to get through to him. I can see the bijass is overtaking him again.

A hot wind blows, picking up bits of sand and carrying it into my eyes. Clenching them tight as they water in reaction, I rub, trying to get the grit out. When I open them, he's not looking at me but staring back into the distance where we've been heading. The wind is still blowing, much harder than normal, causing the fine grains of sand to pelt against me almost painfully.

"Oh no," he says.

"What?" I ask, following his gaze.

My stomach sinks to the ground and bile rises in my throat. A dark, maroon-colored cloud dominates the horizon, rising from the ground what looks like hundreds of feet into the air. It's moving towards us. Drosdan looks around before grabbing me. Sweeping me off my feet, he runs.

"Sandstorm," he says, adjusting me in his arms.

"What are we going to do?" I ask, fear pounding with my racing heart.

"Survive," he hisses.

The wind blows harder, bits of sand slamming against my exposed skin like tiny shards of glass. I squint and see that he's running straight at the oncoming storm. A wall of dark clouds crawls toward us. It looks like some giant erasing everything in its path. I've never felt so scared in all my life. Even when Gershom grabbed power from Rosalind I wasn't this scared. During that I felt at least a modicum of control. The oncoming storm is implacable. There is nothing I can do to stop it or even avoid it. The land around us is flat for as far as I can see, not even a rocky outcropping to use as shelter.

"How?" I ask, my voice cracking. "We need shelter!"

The wind is picking up even more, making it harder to talk. Carrying words away with it.

"I'll find something," he yells to be heard.

"Drosdan, you're running into it, we should turn around."

"No," he says shaking his head. "Our only hope is to get through it."

"Through that!" I scream, shaking in his arms. He pulls me tighter against him.

"Yes," he agrees. "Otherwise we're moving with it, we'll never get out of it."

It doesn't matter that his words make sense. Every fiber of my body is on fire and screaming that we're going the wrong way. Grains of sand are tearing at me, tiny cuts growing from irritations to serious concerns. Clenching my eyes tight I breathe through my nose and place all my trust in him. There's nothing else I can do, but as resolve forms, peace comes with it. The light shining through my tightly clenched eyelids darkens and then the sand is no longer tearing at my skin. When I open my eyes in surprise, it takes a moment for me to realize he's folded his wings around me, forming a protective cocoon.

A sudden gust of wind blasts, and he rocks backwards with the force, clenching me tighter to his chest. Leaning forward, he forces progress against the assault. The sound of sand blasting grows louder until it's all I can hear. The dim light that was coming through fades until I'm enclosed in darkness. My heart pounds in my chest so hard it feels like it might explode. Minutes crawl by, but there is no way to measure the passage of time. There is only the ongoing roar of wind and sand.

"Drosdan," I say but he doesn't respond. He has his head tucked down between his wings, his jaw a hard line just over my head. When he doesn't respond, I say his name again louder. "Drosdan!"

"Yes?" he says, sounding out of breath.

I feel him fighting for each step forward as gusts of wind push back. Unrelenting, he forces progress against impossible odds.

"Can we make it?" I voice the fear sitting in my belly like a cold hand grasping at my vitals.

He doesn't answer for a long moment. My heart pounding in my chest measures the passing moments as I wait for him to answer. He draws in a deep breath then hisses.

"You are my treasure," he says.

Warmth flares in my stomach driving out the chill of fear at his words. They say everything he needs to say, claiming me as his but it's so much more. Back on the ship I don't think any woman would have accepted a man saying such a thing to her, claiming her in such a primal way, but when Drosdan says it, it's different.

He's not just claiming me, he's giving himself to me, fully, and he's mine as much or more than I am his. Shifting my weight, I wrap my arms tighter around him. It's not an answer to my question, but it is all I need. I am his. He will protect me.

The roar of the wind rises, and the sound of sand slamming against his protective wings is deafening. Sympathy pain aches, but I can only imagine what he must be feeling despite his protective scales. My own, unprotected skin would be shredded. Time crawls along measured only by Drosdan's occasional grunt. I don't bother talking because what can I say? I'm helpless in his arms. Even so, I've never felt safer.

10

DROSDAN

*P*ain.

Sand rips across me, tearing and cutting. One step after another. It's all I can do. Can't look, can't see, can't stop.

Must save Sarah.

Her weight in my arms is my rock. Her head on my chest and arms around my neck are all that matters. Have to find shelter.

The bijass swirls around the edges of thought, swelling, pushing in. It offers a kind of respite. The sand tearing across me feels like its stripping everything off me.

Duty. I've run from my duty.

No, he failed me. Failed us. No leader should demand what he did. A leader respects his followers, cares for them. He sent Sarah into danger without backup. He was wrong. That he doesn't see it isn't my problem, it's his.

The fog of the bijass pushes as anger flares white hot. The look on Visidion's face, Rosalind nodding next to him. Betrayal.

There's a lull in the wind, but then it slams into me,

sliding me back. Leaning into it until I'm almost bent in half. Sand cuts my wings shielding her. The pain fuels my rage.

They can't have this. They can't have us.

I've given everything.

Images rise, unbidden, but no, I can't look at them. Memories lost to the fog of the past where they have to stay. Glimpsing an emptiness that yawns like a massive black hole sucking me down. As my feet slide across the sand my thoughts mimic the motion into the clawing blackness.

"Fire!" the General barks the order.

"No," I say, hands shaking, staring at his cold, empty eyes.

"Do as you're told, soldier," he hisses. "Now."

The butt of the rifle against my shoulder becomes the center of my attention. My finger tightening on the trigger. Follow orders. Obey. Obey.

It pounds through me, interwoven into the very essence of what I am. The General looks down on the row of us, his soft yellow skin, dark eyes, and that evil toothy grin. My body betrays me, following his orders no matter how I fight it. I can't stop it.

A woman screams, begging. The men next to me resist too, but we can't fight it.

"NO!" I scream, pushing the memories away.

"Drosdan?" Sarah asks, her voice trembles.

I'm shaking, but I focus on her. Her weight, her arms around my neck, the softness of her body molded against my chest. I should answer her, I try, but can't push words past the pulsing red fog pushing against my thoughts. The sand tears at the delicate membrane of my wings, millions of tiny cuts, each a flash of pain to be pushed past. The wind is so strong I'm taking three steps to make one step forward. Trying to dig my feet into solid ground, desperate for anything to push forward through the next step. There has to be shelter, somewhere.

Can't look past the shield of my wings enclosing us. Her

fingers twine in my hair, running through it, tugging down, then her lips are on mine. Soft, warm, plump and full of life. They pull me through the fog into her. Her tongue grazes across my lips, and I claim it with my own. The outside world fades as she takes her place as the center of my universe. She is all, my treasure. Pouring myself into the kiss, I give myself to her.

"We need shelter," she breathes, breaking the kiss with a gasp.

"Yes," I agree, able to speak at last, the grip of the bijass easing.

The wind drops suddenly, and I stumble. No more is the sand tearing into me. As fast as it hit, we seem to have come out of it. I open my wings just enough to peek out, and I see nothing but empty plains around us. After I fold my wings back, Sarah and I look around an empty, red world overcast with a dim brown light. There are angry, red-brown clouds in the distance. When I set Sarah on her feet, she takes my hand and together we turn in a circle. The clouds surround us on all sides. Overhead it is cloudy, blocking any view of the suns.

"We're in the eye of the storm," Sarah says.

"What does that mean?" I ask.

"It's the center," she explains. "The way the winds blow is circular around a central point—we're in that point."

Closing my protective lenses over my eyes adjusts my sight so I can see further even in the dim light. In the distance are dark shapes. Squinting I try to make out exactly what they are but am unable to. Whatever they are, they will provide some shelter, which is the only hope we have right now.

"There," I say, pointing towards the shapes.

Sarah looks but shakes her head.

"I can't see anything," she says.

"Shapes, something is over there."

"Better than nothing," she says. "We need shelter, anything, because there's a lot more storm to come, I'm guessing."

"I will get us there," I say, sweeping her back into my arms.

I'm running before she can get her arms around my neck and spreading my wings to catch soft air currents that help carry us forward. There's a constant pain from the thousands of cuts and tears, but I have to push that aside. Each time my foot sets down, I push off the ground, pouring everything I have into that step, leaping into the air. Moving my wings to best catch the air, gaining as much altitude as I can from the leap, then gliding forward. It covers a lot of ground fast.

The wind picks up again, twisting around us, shortening how far I glide with each leap. Jumping forward, wings wide, the wind slams into me with a circular force catching my right wing hard. Tendons tear, and I'm spun around, losing control. By swinging my tail I'm able to keep us upright, but I land hard twisting my left knee.

"Ah!" Sarah cries out as we spin and land.

Even though I hold her protectively to my chest, she's jarred as we hit, and her head bounces against me.

"Ugh," I grunt, pain flaring in my knee.

"Are you okay?" Sarah asks.

"I'll be fine," I hiss, pushing myself forward, but now my knee won't take weight easily, and I'm forced to limp.

"Put me down," she demands, shifting her weight.

"It's fine," I growl.

"No, you're hurt!" she says, her voice cracking.

"We don't have time," I reply, each step forward sending a blinding flash of pain.

She wiggles in my arms then I lose my grip, and she drops

to her feet. Stopping, I reach to grab her again, but she holds up a hand and shakes her head.

"Don't be an idiot," she says.

I close my eyes and take a deep breath. She's right. I can't carry her fast enough, and we don't have time. When I don't move, she drops to her knees and leans close to my knee, feeling around it.

"Ow," slips out of me when she grasps my knee between her hands.

"It's sprained, at a minimum," she says. "Can you walk at all?"

"We don't have a choice," I tell her.

"Yeah," she replies, frowning. "Okay, but you can't carry me. I'll run beside you."

"Okay," I agree, a stabbing pain in my chest.

She's right, no matter that I hate it. Anger rises and the red fog of the bijass grabs for control. It almost takes over. If Sarah weren't standing there, eyes filled with concern, jaw tight, lips pursed, I might have lost myself to it. Holding on to her as my anchor, I'm able to resist, barely.

"Let's go," she says, rising up. She puts a hand on my cheek and lifts herself up to plant a fast kiss on my lips. "We have to hurry."

No longer carrying her weight as well as my own helps, but each step is still excruciating. White-hot stabbing sensation from my knee every time I put weight on it. I hobble along, the only advantage is that Sarah is not having problems keeping up with me as we do our best to race across the desert.

Randomly, gusts of wind hit, pushing us off course, but we struggle on, making progress. As the frequency of the gusts increases, the blurs we're heading for become clear. At first I had thought the shapes were rocks that I could only hope would provide us with some shelter but it's more than that. They're buildings. Low, squat ones, but buildings none-theless. A light feeling swells in my stomach as hope blooms.

"Oh, wow," Sarah says before we've gone much further. "Buildings!"

"Yes," I say.

"Did you know they were here?" she asks, panting as we continue our run. Even with my bad knee, she's having to take three steps for every one of mine.

I don't answer her immediately. Did I? Something tugs from deep inside the fog of the bijass. Maybe? A sense of... something. A coldness is behind that feeling, almost a sense of something bad coming or going to happen.

"I don't know," I say, telling her the truth.

"How can you not know?" she asks.

"It's vague," I say. "A memory, partial. It seems familiar somehow."

The closer we get, the more that sense of familiarity grows. Like an itch that's under my scales and therefore impossible to get to.

"Deja vu," she huffs.

"What?" I ask, the word sounding strange. It's not some-thing I've heard before.

"It's a word meaning a feeling that you've been there before," she laughs.

"Yes, that seems to fit," I agree, wincing as I put my leg down wrong, applying too much pressure on my knee.

"We're almost there," Sarah says, touching my arm.

"It's fine," I lie.

The pain is getting worse. White-hot and stabbing with the slightest amount of weight on it. There's no time to slow though, the wind is rising and picking up sand. The eye of this storm, as she called it, will not last, and we'll be back in it again. We race in silence broken only by Sarah's huffing. As we close with the buildings, I see this was once a very small town. Probably there was some valuable thing found here that led to this settlement. Before the devastation, such were common, dotting the landscape between the large cities.

There are five structures standing in a row, while the ruins of others can be seen on either side of and beyond them. The walls of all of them are crumbling, and on three of them the roof has collapsed. One of the middle ones seems to be in the best shape, so I guide us towards it. The wind is blowing harder still, bits of sand being carried with it, abrasive against us. The building holds back some of it, but not all. As we reach the wall, pain flares in my knee and I trip, catching myself on it.

"Are you okay?" Sarah asks, having to shout to be heard.

"I'm fine," I lie.

The pain is a white-hot ball, throbbing constantly, but I don't have time to tend to the wound. Safety is all that matters—hers. Taking her hand, I lead the way around the building. They're close together, forcing me to turn sideways to move between them. Even so, my wings and tail scrape along the rough surfaces as I slide past. We emerge on the far side into an open square blocked out by more of the small buildings. The roofs and walls of most of them are in states of disrepair with large holes through most of them. Some of the holes are obviously from explosions, while others appear to be caused by natural decay.

"There," Sarah says, pointing at a dark opening.

Once there would have been a door over it, but only bits of hanging wood are left. As we step into the darkness inside, the wind blasts up to a high speed, whistling as it passes between the houses. The sky above darkens, making it clear we're barely making it before the next stage of the storm hits.

The interior walls have collapsed, leaving rotting dividers rising about halfway to the ceiling. Once there might have been various rooms, now there is a single space with half walls. The door we entered through is the only source of light as there are no windows. Heavy shadows lie waiting in every corner, a perfect place for predators to hide. Turning to Sarah and grabbing her arms, I move her to stand next to the door with her back against the wall.

"Wait," I say, speaking soft to avoid alarming anything that might be hiding.

Favoring my good leg heavily, I take my lochaber off my back and use it for support. The wind howls outside accented by the sound of sand blasting against the stone walls of the house. Making my way to the first dark corner I stab into it with the blade of my lochaber ready for anything. Swinging it side to side until I'm satisfied nothing is hiding I repeat the action at each spot until I'm certain the house is safe. Only then do I return to Sarah.

"Clear?" she asks, shouting to be heard over the wind.

"Yeah," I answer.

Sand blows in the open door, piling up just over the threshold. The open square is protected by buildings on all side so it's not coming in with force, nothing like what is happening beyond the safety of the house walls but it's annoying so we go to the back taking shelter behind one of the half walls. Sarah rummages up pieces of wood from around the place, piling them up and I use my glands to light a fire for us.

The soft flickering of the orange and yellow light accents her face. Her eyes dance in the firelight with a life that makes my heart skip a beat. She is so perfect and beautiful. Nothing in the world compares to her. A warm, tingling sensation races out from my core through my limbs. Outside the storm rages but here, together, we're safe, for now.

"Turn around," Sarah says, standing before me with her hands on her hips. Instinct says no but one look at her face and I turn without a word.

"It's fine," I say.

"Oh Drosdan," he says, her voice heavy with concern. "We don't have enough water to clean this."

"Don't worry about it," I say. "I'll heal."

"With sand in all your wounds!" she says.

Looking at her over my shoulder a drop of moisture runs down her cheek. Turning I wipe it away with my thumb. She shakes her head side-to-side as another drop falls from her eyes. She throws her hands up in the air as more drops fall. Pain stabs deep into my heart that and it feels like its breaking. Climbing to my knees I wrap my arms around her, pulling her tight and kissing her, wanting nothing more than to take her pain away.

11

SARAH

"Oh, Drosdan," the words catch in my throat looking at his back.

His poor wings are nothing but tiny cuts coated with blood, dirt and sand. My stomach clenches tight.

"It's nothing," he says again, grunting.

"I have to clean the wounds," I tell him.

"I told you we don't have enough water," he says, looking over his shoulder at me. "It will be fine."

The storm continues to rage outside the walls of our shelter. An unending roar that fades to almost a white noise, it's so constant. Helplessness hits me in a wave that makes my knees weak. Drosdan grabs me before I can fall. The wave passes as quick as it came, leaving me shaken. What is wrong with me? I'm stronger than this.

"I'm fine," I say, straightening, but he doesn't let me go.

Looking into his eyes, the bulk of him surrounding me, I become acutely aware of our bodies touching. My nipples stiffen, rubbing against the rough fabric of my shirt almost painfully. His lips, so full, inviting, calling to my own. Slowly, as if time crawls, pausing as each second ticks by and we move closer, I rise up. As our lips touch, molding one to the other, the fire in my core explodes, raging through me.

He hooks his hands under my ass, lifting me up to him, our lips never parting. The taste of him is exotic, enticing, a tangy spiciness that I can't get enough of. Parting my lips, I dart my tongue out and lick them, leaving my tongue tingling. As he lifts me, my nipples drag across the scales of his chest even through the fabric, eliciting an unexpected moan. One of his hands moves up my back and entangles in my hair as we continue our kiss.

Butterflies dance in my stomach, and cold chills run down my arms, every hair standing on end. He molds my body against the hard muscle of his chest, while the bulge in his pants digs into my stomach, calling to me. He turns, pressing me between him and a wall. Running my fingers through his hair, I dart my tongue out, tasting his lips, and his tongue seeks out mine. As they touch, my heart skips, and I gasp. Pinning me with his waist to the wall, his hands are free to roam up and down my thighs, leaving trails of fire in the wake of their passage. His massive erection pushes hard against my pussy. The pressure on my clit is overwhelming.

He drives his tongue past my lips, penetrating my mouth vigorously, in the same way I want his cock to penetrate me lower, past my more delicate lips. His tongue explores my mouth, dancing with mine, and as it thrusts in and out of my mouth, his hips move back and forth, rubbing in and out against the pounding need between my legs. I moan into his mouth, desire taking over and pushing out all other thoughts. Running my hands over his massive, bulging chest muscles makes my fingers tingle, electric. The edges of his scales are rough, but each one individually is smooth as glass. It's an intriguing dichotomy that delights my senses as I move my hands over them.

Our tongues wrestle as his hands top my thighs, and he

slowly drags them up my sides to the undersides of my breasts. My nipples throb as he moves closer to them, begging for attention. He slips his hands under my blouse, touching my bare skin. Heat flushes from that point of soft contact. Groaning, I thrust my hips hard against him, causing his massive erection to move against my clit. Pleasure explodes in response, blinding me with its intensity.

Hands cupping my breasts his thumbs flick my nipples creating a new explosion of pleasure that rocks my world. His tongue doesn't stop as his hands work my tits and his hard cock rubs up and down through the layers of fabric still teasing my clit.

He clasps his hands on my tits, breaks our kiss, and then his lips and tongue tease their way across my cheek and down my shoulder to my collarbone. Throwing my head back, I drink in the sensation of his attention. His rough tongue leaves goosebumps in its trail as he works his way across my exposed skin.

His hands work my breasts as he kisses across my shoulder, then he grabs my shirt and pulls it over my head. As my breasts fall free between the two of us, the nipples graze across his chest, and I cry out in surprise and pleasure. He grabs my ass and lifts me up higher, holding me there easily. Taking each nipple in his mouth he lavishes the care of his rough tongue on them. The hard points overload with his attention. My hands twine in his hair, pulling as sensation overloads me.

He moves back and forth between my tits, never leaving one for long before returning to it. I drive a hand down between us and into my pants. Finding my throbbing clit I rub and tease it while his tongue works my nipples. He pulls me tightly against him, turning us, and then lowers himself to his knees. He gently lays me down onto the ground, his hands loosen my pants and slide them off. When I reach for his pants, he catches my hands in one of his, and then moves them somewhat roughly over my head, holding them there easily. He's between my legs, leaving me exposed. His eyes drift over me, filled with gleaming lust as he looks me up and down.

As his eyes drift to my intimate parts, I feel suddenly self-conscious. I haven't 'groomed' in over a year, and it's more than obvious. There hasn't been time or opportunity since the wreck of the ship for such self-care.

Holding my arms over my head, he lowers himself to me and kisses me. Pushing aside my self-doubts, I give myself to the kiss. It'll be fine; sex is sex.

He kisses my cheek, then down my neck. As he passes lower, the doubts return in full force. He's passing my breasts and kissing down my stomach. I try to push them aside, try to control them, but I can't. As he lowers himself between my legs, I pull his hair, stopping him. He looks up at me, confusion on his face, and all I can do is bite my lip and shake my head no.

"What's the matter?" he asks.

"I'm…" I can't say the words, my face flushes hot.

He climbs back up, holding himself over me, staring into my eyes.

"What is it Sarah?" he asks.

Shrugging I struggle to say the words, but I'm so embarrassed, my throat feels like its clenched tightly closed.

"I need to… trim," I say, forcing the words out at last.

He nods, kisses me, and then climbs to his feet. He goes over to his pack and begins digging in it. He gets out a bowl, the water bottle, and then a small blade. Sitting up, a cold chill forms in my stomach, and I pull my knees up to my chest. He pours water in the bowl, then places it on top of the fire.

"What are you doing?" I ask.

He looks at me and smiles.

"As you wish," he says.

He takes the bowl of water off of the fire and sets it over next to me. Kneeling in front of me with a small blade in his hand, he stares into my eyes. I don't know what to do or say. He smiles, reaching out with his free hand, touching my face.

"Drosdan," I say, not sure what I'm going to follow his name up with.

"Trust me," he says, voice soft, smiling.

His fingers trace along my jawline, and my heart stops pounding as he does. A calmness comes with his touch, and in that moment I give myself to him fully. Relaxing, I let go of my knees and open my legs to him. He sets to work. There's a level of trust I've never imagined myself giving to anyone. He uses the warm water to wet everything then the knife moves in his steady hand. A small part of me screams as he approaches my delicateness with a sharp blade, but I shut that ignorant primal part of my mind down. His hand is steady, smooth, and careful.

He works quickly, or so it seems, trimming with seamless strokes. He's close, so close I feel his hot breath. It's erotic and arousing in strange ways. He's so close to me, more than just oral, he's inspecting, working carefully. His thumb moves over my lips checking the quality of his work. Looking up from between my legs, he sets the knife aside and smiles as he moves closer and closer. I'm soaking wet and ready as he drops lower, then his hot tongue drags from the bottom of my opening to the top.

A shudder races through me and I gasp. My heart rate triples, and instinctively I grab his hair. He moans into me, and a new shudder races up my spine as his warm breath passes across my wet lips. His tongue drives through my soft folds, exploring every delicate piece. His attention is so complete, so full, I lose myself to the sensations of his pleasuring. In and out he drives his tongue, impossibly deep into me, swirling and moving in ways that feel impossible. The sensations are overwhelming. My core tightens until almost of their own accord, my hips are bucking up into him, driving him deeper into me.

Pulling back, he traces the edges of my lips on each side, then drives his tongue through until it is pressing hard against my clitoris. The roughness of his tongue on my sensitive nub pushes me over the edge. Crying out my pleasure, hands knotted in his hair, I scream his name and thrust into him. He grabs my ass, holding me tight against him, moving his head up and down. Muscles contract, my throat clenches tight, my back arches, and shudders take over as the orgasm rages through me. As it passes, I relax into his hold, and the last shockwaves race through until I'm jelly in his arms where he holds me up by my hips.

Gently he lays me down. My breath slows as my heart rate returns to normal. He hovers over me, watching, waiting for it to pass with the patience only an attentive and conscientious lover could have. He's in no hurry to claim his pleasure now that he's given me mine. Touching his face, I trace his full lips with my fingers, pushing my index past them into his mouth, tracing his teeth. His tongue darts out, licking my finger, and I moan. My free hand runs through his hair while my index explores his mouth. Holding himself up with one arm, he frees the tie of his pants with the other and pushes them down. Looking down across myself, I get my first view of his cock as his pants drop away.

I've known about the Zmaj cocks for a while but haven't seen one myself. Even from what the other girls have said, I'm thinking that Drosdan's cock is as impressive as his overall size is, in comparison to the other men. It's huge, and I do mean huge—with a solid guess he's bigger than most of the other Zmaj in this way too.

I don't think I could encircle it in both my hands even without the ridges. I know my body will adapt to it, after all a woman's body is made to push out babies, which are as big as a watermelon, and he's not that large. We'll just have to take it slow, something I know that Drosdan would do anyway.

He sucks on my finger in his mouth while I take my other hand out of his hair and run it down, across his body, to find his cock. Touching it lightly, I stroke the soft underneath of it. It jumps up at my touch, somehow becoming even stiffer. My smile grows, seeing his cock react to me. A warm, fuzzy sensation spreads across me as I continue to stroke it with a delicate touch. He moans around my finger that he's still sucking on, and he takes my left tit in his hand and circles the hard nipple with his thumb. As his thumb passes over my erect nipple I gasp then groan. Electrical sensations racing out from that sensitive point.

His hips rock forward then back a little, pushing down then pulling back from my touch. His eyes are closed, his head tossed back, and his tongue strokes my finger in his mouth. Gripping his cock the best I can, I pull forward, guiding him towards my waiting wetness.

He moves with my pull until the head of his massive member is at my opening, ready to penetrate. Letting go of his cock I press hard against my clit and rub fast circles. Desire roars to life as I touch myself and my body responds. Wetness forms on my delicate lips, making me better prepared for his girth.

Grabbing the head of his cock, I hook my hand behind the first ridge on the top and use it as a grip to pull him forward. Even the head of his cock stretches me as it passes my outer lips.

"Ah!" I gasp as it penetrates, pushing aside the delicate parts and forcing me to expand to accommodate it.

He stops instantly, eyes opening, pulling my finger out of his mouth.

"Are you okay?" he asks.

Biting my lower lip, I nod. The sensation is too much for me to form words around. It's pleasure with a hint of pain and so overwhelming, so much what I want and need, I can't process it logically. He holds himself, not moving, until at last I push my hips towards him, forcing him deeper.

The first ridge reaches me and my body stops him from progressing. Pausing I let it adjust and he waits, leaving me in control. Panting, sensations rushing through me in waves followed by waves, my body shifts and accepts his girth. Once that settles, I push forward. The ridge passes into me, and my pussy expands. Nerves that have never been touched are set alight with the fire of sensation and pleasure. A warmth of blood rushes through my core, then overloads thought with blinding pleasure. Distantly I hear myself crying out his name but it's like that's another person making those sounds. I'm surrounded by pleasure and sensation. A universe of color that claims me separate from my body.

Instinct, primal and pure, takes over as I take his huge cock with its ridged top deep into my body. Eventually it hits the bottom, and only that stops him from claiming me. I give myself to him in ways I never imagined possible. Our bodies joining as one as we find a rhythm together. He moves in and out as I rise and fall from him. Merging our bodies into one, pleasure joining us at the hips and more.

His lips find mine and we kiss. Up and down, in and out, we fall into each other over and over. Losing myself in the beats of the motion. His hearts beating against my chest, falling into time with mine. Our breaths match each other, growing faster as we both build to a new climax.

He thrusts in again and holds.

"SARAH-H-H-H!" he screams, a hissing to the end of my

name as he drags it out holding himself deep inside my eager pussy.

As he pumps his seed inside me, I grip him tightly, holding myself against him, moaning with the force of the orgasm ripping through my own body.

At last I collapse to the ground, and he lies down on top of me, breathing heavily. His soft kisses pull me back to the world, along with the touch of his hands running through my hair. As I become aware, his beautiful eyes stare into mine, and I return his kisses. His cock softens inside me as we lie there together, holding each other.

Our first time was more than I ever imagined.

He pulls his soft cock out, and I know what's coming next. I'm ready for it as his secondary cock rises to the occasion.

12

DROSDAN

*M*y arm is numb. When I move to stretch, Sarah murmurs softly. Her head rests on my shoulder, and she shifts, one hand moving across my chest and throwing a leg across me. Reaching with my free arm, I grab the blanket and pull it over us. The air is cool, for Tajss at least. Watching her chest rise and fall with even, regular movement, a swelling starts in my chest and expands until it feels like I'll explode. A lightness fills me, an airy, strange sensation that radiates from a glowing warmth deep inside my core. My inner dragon hums with satisfaction, knowing that my treasure has accepted me. She is mine as I am hers. We are as it should be.

Nothing could feel better than her in my arms.

The storm is over. There is no sound except that of her breathing. Her heart beats against my chest, slow and steady, thumping strong against me. Thoughts flit through, things I should do, concerns and worries about what comes next but I push all of that aside. This moment, right now, here with her, everything is perfect. Everything else that is to come will be there when it is there.

It takes an effort of will to quiet thoughts of the future, but once I do the quiet settles over me. Closing my eyes, I focus on the sensation of her. The points of contact between our bodies are warm, and her soft skin is so enticing. So different than a Zmaj female, who would also be covered with scales, as I am. Her breasts, so open, boldly thrusting out to the world as all the human females' do, are an endless sense of wonder to me. A Zmaj female's breasts are covered with protective plates and are only exposed for feeding children.

The sensation of her soft mounds against my side hold my attention, and my cock stirs, giving a jump of interest as my attention focuses on them.

Pulling my attention from that single point of contact, I focus on each point of contact, where her hips rest against me down to her leg lying across mine. Idly I touch her hair and run my fingers through its silky softness. She stirs once more, and I stop, not wanting to wake her. I don't want this moment to end, ever. This is what I've needed and wanted but never knew. Life since the devastation has been one day after another, surviving, because that is what I do. Living more for Visidion and the Tribe than for myself. Living with no hope, no purpose, knowing, whether any of us admitted it or not, that there was no future for our race. We had no females, no hope of a next generation. When we died it would be the end of the Zmaj.

It was life, and life finds a way. Ignoring the grimness of the situation, or at least refusing to look at it, we continued. The arrival of the humans changed everything. I was little more than a primal animal, operating on instinct alone, holding onto the last vestiges of humanity by clinging to the Edicts as a lifeline between myself and the endless rage of the bijass. Now I am a male again. A Zmaj warrior, as I once was.

A warrior.

Yes, I was a warrior. A cold chill races through me at the thought. Why? What happened?

The memories are buried deep in the bijass, hidden away and somehow I know that I don't want them. I don't want to remember. If I do something terrible will happen. I can't look at it.

"Mmmm," Sarah murmurs, shifting against me. Her breasts move along my side and my cock rises to greet her standing tall and erect as she stretches against me. "Well, morning."

She laughs, turning her head up away from my erection to meet my eyes. Tilting her head back, she puckers her lips and I meet them with a kiss.

"Good morning," I reply.

"Happy to see me?" she giggles.

"You are my treasure," I say.

"Mm," she grins.

She rises onto an elbow, then slides over and across me, rising up until she's positioned over my erection. Slowly she lowers herself onto my hardness. She's wet and warm. At the same time as the head of my cock enters her, a sigh rips out of me. It's like coming home. Everything that is wrong with the world becomes right as our bodies join.

She throws her head back and gasps as she makes it down to the first ridge of my cock. By shifting her hips from side to side and then rotating, she works her way over the ridge. It enters her with a sensation of a pop that makes my cock spasm as it enters the tight, wet tunnel of her love. The intensity of sensation is enough to test my resolve and push me towards a climax long before I'm ready to give to such.

Reaching up I grab her soft mounds, cupping each of them in a hand and teasing her puffy nipples to hard points with my thumbs.

She throws her head back moaning, her hands covering

mine. She lowers herself further, slowly, taking each ridge of my cock one at a time until I'm fully seated inside of her. Biting her lower lip, eyes closed, she rotates a slow, small circle. The sensations are overwhelming. I can't keep my own eyes open, moaning, my hips push up against her almost of their own accord. Instinct and need drive my body more than any conscious thought. The warm wetness surrounding my cock as she rises up off then drives herself down onto me.

"Ah!" she cries out as she drives down.

"Sarah!" I scream her name.

Her hands find my face, tracing the line of my jaw as he hips work up and down on my cock. Trailing my fingers across her collarbone then tracing the line of her waist on either side, I find her ass and give it a playful slap. She moans in response, and my cock stiffens even harder.

She rises and falls on my cock until I find myself raising to meet her incoming descent and pulling back as she does. Our breathing falls into time with each other, my hearts pound in my chest, and I'm panting as I focus on staving off the building climax. Concentrating, I push it back, watching her through slitted eyes I can barely keep open, I see her pleasure building. Her eyes roll up in her head, she bites her lip harder, and then her hands clench into fists on my chest as she drives herself down, taking my cock fully and deeply inside her. She throws her head back and cries out a wordless sound as she gives herself to the orgasm. Her body stiffens, her back arches more, then I throw myself over the edge with her and my come explodes out, pumping into her.

She pants, moans, and I'm doing the same as my cock pumps stream after stream into her. The orgasm lasts longer than anything I've experienced.

"Yes, yes, yes," she pants softly as spasms continue to wrack her body with the aftershocks of her climax.

She collapses onto my chest, breathing heavily while lying on top of me. Encircling her in my arms, I hold her while my cock softens inside of her warmth. After a time she shifts, rising onto her elbows, then leaning in and kissing me with her soft, perfect, full lips.

"Good morning," she grins.

"Definitely," I answer, running my fingers through her hair.

She rolls off of me, holding her head up on an elbow so she is looking at me. She runs a hand down her side then cups her sex.

"Damn, you're so big," she laughs.

"Did I hurt you?" I ask, concern rising.

"No, but I do feel well... satisfied," she says, arching an eyebrow and shaking her head.

"And that is a good thing?" I ask.

"Oh yeah," she says, leaning in for another kiss and cutting off any further words.

"We should get moving," I say after an extended period of kissing.

"And do what? We've run away from all our responsibilities," she says and only because I know her so well do I hear the hint of regret in those words.

"We need to explore this village, establish supplies, fortify a shelter and see what resources we have available."

"Sure," she sighs, sitting up. "If you insist."

I smile and shake my head. A stray ray of light coming through a small hole in the roof hits her hair. It highlights her to perfection, and I can't tear my eyes away from her. It outlines her with a glow that makes her look like a heavenly body somehow come to Tajss. I was never, that I recall, a religious male, but in her I have something I can worship. My treasure, the other half of me, the missing piece that makes life worth having.

"What?" she asks, noticing me staring at her.

"You're perfect," I say, my voice soft.

Her beautiful face becomes even more so as it flushes with a hint of red that makes her eyes alight as she quickly looks down shaking her head. She clasps her shirt to her chest, covering herself, but it only makes her more attractive. Hiding the nipples, but it draws my attention to the cleavage, where her breasts are pushed together by her crossed arms. The line from her shoulders down to her arms, the way she tilts her head, the sunlight casting light and shadows nothing could be more beautiful. My secondary cock stiffens, standing erect between us.

"You're insatiable," she laughs seeing it.

"It's you," I answer her honestly. "I can't get enough of you."

"Thank you," she says, shaking her head side to side. "But you're right, we should set about setting ourselves up while the suns are up. There will be time enough for that later."

I can't argue with her, though the pounding in my secondary cock wants me to. Climbing to my feet, I pull my pants on, but can't help noticing her watching as they pass over my cock. I pause for dramatic effect, letting it hang out longer than is necessary, half-hoping she'll change her mind. She bites her lip, and I know she's thinking about it, but then she tears her eyes away.

Damn, she's right though.

After tying my pants, I kneel next to my pack and close it up before slinging it over a shoulder. Then I grab my lochaber and go to the makeshift door we covered over and remove the barrier. Piled-up sand pours into the building as I remove it, and we have to step over it to emerge into the bright red suns of Tajss.

"There must have been a water source, possibly hidden inside one of these buildings," I say pointing around us.

"These villages are always built around water and usually near some other thing of value."

"Oh, well that's good," she says.

"Maybe," I say.

"Maybe?" she asks.

"There would have been one here when it was founded, but that doesn't mean what was here survived the Devastation," I answer her.

"Damn, yeah," she says. "Well, water will be first then."

We go to the first building and start exploring. I go in to each of them first, lochaber at the ready. It's hard telling what might have taken up residence in any of these buildings. The first three we enter are empty of any life, but there are a few useful things we gather and carry back to the building we have chosen as home. Pieces of wood, some cookware, and a few shards of pottery. The fourth is on the opposite side of the square. As I push the remnants of the broken door aside, something stirs inside. Holding a hand back to keep Sarah from stepping close, I wait and listen. No other sound comes, so I glance at her holding up my closed fist. I stare into her eyes until she nods understanding.

Stepping to the opposite side of the door opening, I stare into the dim light inside hoping to see the source of the noise. Nothing. Using my lochaber, I thrust it inside hoping the motion will attract whatever is waiting. Again nothing happens. Ducking to avoid hitting my head, I step through the door, eyes darting around, blinking rapidly to adjust to the dimmer light.

A shadow moves to my left, and I whirl towards it, bringing the lochaber to a defensive position. Something whines, a sound that tugs at some distant, forgotten memory. Keeping the lochaber ready, I step forward, prepared to thrust. Something darts out of the shadow in a blur, moving along the wall. When I swing at the motion there's a mewling sound accenting the whistle of the blade cutting through the air. It's moving too fast to see what it is clearly. I turn on my heel, tracking, but it runs along the wall and towards the door.

Thrusting, I miss again, but it mewls loudly. Sarah is in the doorway, looking in. My heart leaps into my throat—the thing is running towards her.

"Run!" I scream, fear gripping my entire body in cold chills as I thrust my blade at the blur again.

It leaps into the air, jumping over my thrusting blade, but also towards Sarah. Her eyes widen and her arms come up, but she's too slow. It's going to hit her. Time slows to a crawl. Pulling my blade back and turning, I push it forward again, but I'm also too slow. The blur hits Sarah and she stumbles backwards out of my sight. I hear her crying out. I'm running forwards, but it feels like the air itself is working against me. Can't move fast enough, can't get to her. She's crying out— she needs me. That thing has her, and it's going to die. She is mine, my treasure. I must save her.

Emerging from the door, hissing my rage. Sarah is on her back, and the thing is on top of her. She's rolling from side to side, struggling. Raising the lochaber back, I swing it with all I've got, intending to cut the thing in half.

"NO!" Sarah screams.

It's hurting her, and I have to stop it. She looks at me, the smile on her face turning to horror. She rolls, taking the thing with her, rolling out of the way of my blade.

"Sarah, hold still!" I yell.

"No! Wait," she cries out.

Stopping mid-swing at her command, the blade quivers in mid-air between us. She's laughing. The thing on her chest, a hair ball, rests in her arms. She's holding it tight against her as she rises to her feet. Now that it's still, I get my first good look at it. It has four legs, a small, compact body covered with yellow fur that has a reddish tint and dark stripes that would allow it to blend in with the sands of Tajss. It turns its head and looks at me with eyes that are a deep emerald green. It opens its mouth revealing rows of tiny, sharp teeth and a tiny pink tongue. A long tail swishes back and forth and it mewls. Along its side, folded tight against it and blending in with the fur are wings.

"It's a kedi," I say.

"A what?" Sarah asks, then she's laughing because it licks her face.

"A kedi," I say again.

"It's cute," she says, scratching it between its pointed ears. "Can we keep it?"

Twirling the lochaber I slide it into its harness and cross my arms over my chest. The kedi licks her face then makes a low grumbling noise. Somehow I know that sound means it's pleased. Some distant memory of a different time.

"As you wish," I say, shaking my head.

Pushing aside intangible misgivings I move to the next house and continue our exploration. Sarah sets the kedi down and it follows her.

13

SARAH

"Come on, Picard," I urge my kedi.

She stares at me then, I swear by all the stars, slowly shakes her head like she knows exactly what I want her to do and is telling me to take a leap. Frowning, I glare at her, and it looks like she grins. She raises a paw and places it on her forehead, like she's face palming me, which is why I came up with her name. Swearing a not-so-nice word, I throw my hands up and turn my back on her. Drosdan turns away quickly, but not quick enough for me to miss he was watching.

"We should gather more water," he says.

"You were watching," I accuse. He glances at me, then looks away shaking his head. "Don't try denying it, I saw you. What is wrong with her?"

"It's a kedi," he says, as if that is all the answer there is to the world or it actually tells me anything.

We didn't have kedi on the ship. Pets were a luxury that only the top-ranked, most wealthy could afford. They weren't common even though they were there. Enough that once we'd landed the breeds could be mated but their population was strictly controlled. There weren't enough resources to let them breed without strict rules.

"And?" I prompt.

He shrugs, glances again, but looks past me at the animal.

"I don't know," he says, shaking his head. "I don't think I like them. Or liked them."

He hates admitting that he's lost chunks of his memory. Knowing that it was a big admission for him to say anything to that effect, I let it drop. Turning to face the kedi, I arch an eyebrow at her, then decide she's going to do whatever the hell she wants anyway and give up. Drosdan has our water bottle and a pot in his hand as he leaves our home, so I fall in with him.

We've been here for three weeks and life is finding a rhythm, as it does. We've passed the days exploring the village and working on creating basic comforts. Stepping out of our home into the hot, double suns, I squint against the glare and follow him. The village is a series of interlinked squares, all the homes facing in toward each other, eight buildings, two each side-by-side form the pattern. Between the two side-by-side buildings is a walkway which leads to the next square. There are fourteen such squares that comprise this village. Drosdan says it's a small village by Zmaj standards but it's plenty large enough for a community.

Drosdan is heading between two of the buildings towards the water source we found, which is two squares over. Rushing over, I catch up to him and follow him through the next square. His tail swishes back and forth, holding my attention as the scales running down it reflect the sunlight, casting tiny rainbows into the air. His wings rustle, and the muscles of his back shift as he moves. It's a gorgeous, enticing sight watching him just walk. The strength he displays even in the way he moves holds my attention. It helps distract me from the gnawing worries that eat at me.

Every day I think of her. I betrayed her trust, left my duty behind to follow Drosdan out here into the wilds. Well, technically I didn't follow him, he kidnapped me but semantics, right? It's not like I was unwilling to go, at least not in the moment.

Staying in Gershom's camp was a personal hell. One I endured for Rosalind.

Which is why it bothers me. I did it for her because I believe in her. Her vision of the future, her leadership—she is the only hope we have of surviving. No one else is thinking in the terms Rosalind does. It's not about surviving today or even this year. It's about surviving in the next generation and the one after that. That's the picture no one else is looking at. We're all so busy with the day-to-day that none of us were looking past it. Rosalind did, though, and I know she's right to have done so. We won't survive on our own.

Lost in my thoughts and struggling with regrets, I bump into Drosdan.

"Hey," I exclaim, looking up.

He's standing stock still, staring into the square before us. When he doesn't respond, I step around the side of him, so I can see his face. His eyes are unfocused, staring at the empty space. When I snap my fingers in front of his face, he doesn't even blink.

"Drosdan?" I ask, doing my best to keep the quiver out of my voice, but it's there.

Still he doesn't respond. Cold chills race down my spine and along my limbs. Goosebumps form on my skin in their passage. Cupping his cheek in my hand, I rise up onto my toes trying to meet his eyes more directly. It's a futile task because he's so much taller than I, but it's all I've got.

"Hey!" my voice is shrill.

A mewling sound echoes off the nearby walls as Picard pads her way towards me. He opens his wings, stretching his front legs out and arching his back while opening his mouth wide as if yawning then walks over to Drosdan's tail. He bats the tip of it back and forth in a playful manner.

"Yeah, helpful," I say, shaking my head fear growing stronger. "I can't do this without you, what the hell is going on, Drosdan?"

He blinks looking down.

"What is it?" he asks.

"You were… staring," I say unsure what to say.

"Oh," he says and a shudder runs through him. "Sorry."

"Drosdan, what's going on?"

"I don't know," he says, staring over my head. "Something about this place tugs at me."

"What do you mean?"

"I'm not sure," he says, looking into my eyes and smiling. "It's nothing, let's go."

It's obvious he's unwilling to talk about this further, so we continue along the path for water. The building that has water in it is as non-descript as everything else here. All the low, squat buildings look the same on the outside. When we enter this one, pipes are visible coming up out of the ground and through the walls. Some of them drip water, which we tested and found to be potable, so we've set up collectors under the various pipes. Picard makes his way to one of the pieces of tin we're using for that purpose, and his pink tongue starts lapping up some water.

"Do you miss it?" Drosdan asks.

"Miss what?"

He looks over his shoulder at me but doesn't say anything. I know what he means, but I don't know how to answer him. Yes? No? Sort of?

Truth is, I feel bad. I had a duty, and I left it without

warning or word to Rosalind. The people who followed Gershom have to be suffering worse than ever, and their odds of survival drop with every passing day. They were barely surviving when I was there, and I was supplementing the dwindling supplies—with Drosdan's help, of course. It's been long enough now that the supplies have to be almost gone. None of them are hunters, and they have no regular source of water.

"Yes," I say, meeting his gaze at last and owning it.

He nods but doesn't say anything as he fills the water jug. As he steps outside I follow him, waiting to see if he's going to say more. My thoughts linger around those I left behind. Are they still alive? Gershom hadn't been seen in public for a long time, and I wondered if he wasn't sick. No one was really leading his followers, and the culture was decaying fast. As resources dwindled, it can only have gotten worse.

"We made the right choice," Drosdan says over his shoulder.

"Did we?" I ask.

We've avoided this conversation, and that's been okay until now. Now that it's started, the thoughts that I've been suppressing are raging and demanding my attention.

"Yes," he says, turning slowly around.

Staring, I wait for him to continue, but he doesn't.

"How do you mean? What if we were wrong? What if we left them there to die?" I ask.

"We should work on the side of the house more," he says, walking away.

I follow in silence but inside a storm rages. I can't get past the survivors that I left behind. Survivors, victims is a better epithet. Most, maybe not all but the majority of them are scared. Having lived among them, I get it now, where before I never could, not when I was on the outside.

They're only now starting to come to terms with the fact

that there won't be a rescue from Earth. They've lived this long in denial, and some of them are still in it. Stuck here on a planet where everything is trying to kill you, their entire world ripped away, friends and family lost. Of course they're scared. We all were, and anyone who claims they weren't is a liar, a fool, or both. Does their fear mean they deserve to die?

No.

They don't. Scared or fools it doesn't matter—they don't deserve to die. Forgetting Rosalind's view that we need them, which we do, if we're to increase our odds of long-term survival on the planet. They're humans. Simple, driven by impulses beyond their control, but humans.

Drosdan enters our home, and I hear him putting the water away. I stand outside the door waiting on him. Picard weaves his way between my legs rubbing up against me and rustling his wings as he does so. It's distracting and more than a bit annoying, but I've learned that Picard does what Picard wants, and any attempt to dissuade him is an exercise in futility.

When Drosdan reemerges from the house he stops and we lock gazes.

"We should go back," I say. His jaw tightens and his tail twitches faster, sure signs he's irritated. Placing a hand on one hip and holding the other up between us I stop anything he's going to say. "Now, wait, listen."

He arches an eyebrow, staring at me silent, waiting for me to make my argument.

"We can't just leave them there to die," I say.

"It was their choice," he responds.

"Sure," I say. "They chose, but they didn't choose because they're rational. They're scared Drosdan. Hell we're all scared."

"I'm not," he says.

"No, not you, probably not any of the Zmaj, not anymore. I mean the humans. We're scared. Hell, I'm scared right now."

"No," he says, closing faster than I can blink and taking me in his arms. "You have nothing to fear."

His massive size engulfs me, making me feel small. Laying my head against his chest, I wrap my arms around him the best I can. He's too big for me to fully embrace.

"I know I don't," I say, my voice muffled by him. "But we can't leave them."

"They're not our problem," he hisses.

Raising my head from his chest, I look up at him.

"Seriously?" I ask, surprise shocking me. I didn't expect him to agree but I didn't expect him to be dismissive.

"Yes," he says.

"We can't!" I exclaim.

"Yes, we can," he says.

He pushes away and glares, then crosses his arms over his chest while his tail lashes back and forth, betraying his agitation.

"No," I shake my head. "No, that's not who we are. That's not me. I can't do this."

"All my life I've followed orders," he says. "I'm done. They've made their choice. We've made ours. It's done."

"So they're just screwed because they made a bad choice?" I snap.

"Yes," he says, his jaw tight.

My mouth drops open and my mind goes blank. I can't even begin to think with this. Drosdan's steely gaze stares at me as if he's willing me into submission. My face burns hot as anger rages like an inferno. My hands ball into fists, my jaw snaps shut, and I meet his hard stare with one of my own.

"No," I say, fists on hips.

Neither of us say a word. Unblinking we stare at each

other until my eyeballs are burning with the effort, but still I won't look away. This is stupid. Beyond stupid. Glaring at each other until he shakes his head and walks past me out of the house. Turning and watching him go, an empty sensation overtakes me and tears well in my eyes. I can't believe this is happening.

14

DROSDAN

Storming out of the house, I take long strides to leave the square we've made our home and emerge out onto the empty desert. The empty land between the horizon and me stretches as far as I can see.

The bijass is a storm raging in my head. Waves of anger crashing against rational thought, pushing and pulling, dragging me down. It's stupid, all of it. I can't believe she wants to go back for them. I took her away because it was for the best. Rosalind and Visidion sent her on a suicide mission. No matter what pretty words they put on it that's the truth.

No one can believe that Gershom's followers have a chance of survival on their own.

No, they knew what they were sending her into. I'm right, and I know it. Why doesn't she see it?

My hearts pound in my chest, and the edges of my vision cloud with red. Slamming one fist into my hand, I pace back and forth. There has to be an answer. How do I make her see the truth? The rage continues to build; I can't get ahead of it. I run into the desert, hoping to channel the anger into something, anything.

Running gives an outlet, and I pour everything into it.

Images flash out of the encroaching fog of the bijass. Random pictures coming and going without context. Disjointed and making no sense.

Bodies strewn between buildings. Buildings I recognize now as the village Sarah and I are staying in.

Riding on a transport, armored, other armored males with me. The General at the head turning and barking orders at us.

Standing at attention, staring at a line of males armed with mining tools. All the soldiers and I bringing our weapons to bear. The general screaming.

Flash, a bright white flash.

Never again. Never. I can't let it happen.

A scream cuts through all the images flashing through my thoughts, pulling me up short. Straight ahead is a cherepakh, a massive creature close to the size of one of the houses. It's rusty brown, with a hard shell that covers its back and sides, a long neck that emerges from the front of its hard shell with a hooked beak and tiny, beady eyes. It screeches again, a loud, trumpeting sound that assaults my ears.

Reaching over my shoulder, my hand grasps empty air where my lochaber should be. Fear makes my stomach clench tight. The monster paws the ground in front of it, each time its massive foot comes down causes small quakes that vibrates through the earth. It's staring, challenging me.

My anger rages forth as the animal tries to establish dominance. Standing straighter, I spread my wings wide and raise my tail up straight while throwing my arms out.

"Bring it," I hiss.

The cherepakh bobs its head up and down, then trumpets again. I take a step forward, leaning in, increasing my threat. Red closes around me as the monster and I enter a primal battle of dominance. It stomps the ground, bobbing its head, then trumpets its challenge. Spreading my wings out fully, I charge without waiting. Anger pulses with every beating of my hearts, pounding in my head, muscles thrumming with anticipation. Feet meeting the hard resistance of the ground as I charge. The monster charges forward too. Thick legs sticking out of its shell, scrambling across the desert, we race towards each other.

As it comes closer, I leap into the air, wings flapping, fist pulled back. Arcing down, I swing as it raises its head towards me on its long neck. The sharp point of its beaked mouth opens, ready to snap down with bone-breaking force. Twisting to avoid its snapping jaw, I slam a fist into its left eye. The creature cries out in pain, pulling away, and I land in a crouch next to it. One massive leg kicks into me, and I'm knocked backwards, air rushing out of my lungs.

Landing on my back, I tumble head over heels, coming to a stop face-down, sliding across the hard ground. The ground vibrates as the monster rushes towards me, bouncing me up and down. No time to catch my breath, I leap to my feet struggling to inhale. It's closing fast, forcing me to dive to the side to avoid its charge. As I leap to the side, something hits my feet, making me spin through the air. Hitting the ground, I'm sliding along once more. Tiny bits of sand and pebbles worm their way between my scales and tear at me.

Rising to my knees, I see the cherepakh is slow to turn, its forward momentum enforced by its massive weight. It gives me a moment to catch my breath before it turns and charges again. Eyes narrowing, jaw tightening, I clench a fist and wait for it to close. This monster is mine.

When it's so close I can smell the rotten flesh on its breath, I leap forward, grabbing it around the neck just under its head. It screeches, rearing its head back and swinging me around. Flapping my wings and swinging my tail, I'm able to maneuver my way onto the back of its neck. Bouncing up and down as it continues its charge, I dig my fingers into the soft flesh of its exposed neck, but can't get a grip. It twists back and forth, bucking as it tries to shake me off. Scrambling with all I've got, I grip with my legs, slamming my tail down onto its neck repeatedly.

It cries out in frustration and pain, but then it drops its head to the ground and somehow bucks up. Losing my grip, I'm thrown over its head and flying through the air. Spreading my wings I try to gain control of my fall, but pain explodes in my tail.

"AGH!" I cry out as the pain blinds me.

It passes quickly, but I'm swung back and forth. My spine cracks multiple times as it tosses me back and forth, shaking me without mercy. Curling into a ball, I swing at its head, striking it with my fist. It opens its mouth in response, and I'm free, flying once more through the air. Tucking my chin, I land and roll with more control than the last time, coming to my feet. Blood leaks from my tail where it had me, but there is no time for that. The thing looks at me, stomps its foot, and charges.

If I had my lochaber this would go more in my favor, without it my options are limited. I can't let it get close to the houses—it would put Sarah at risk. Have to lead it away.

I run towards it. It lowers its head, mouth snapping with a loud clacking sound as its hard beak opens and closes. At the last possible moment I dart to the side, running past it. The cherepakh skids, flat feet trying to bring it to a stop. Watching it over my shoulder, I keep running while making sure its attention is on me. It turns, good.

Coming to a stop myself, I turn and meet its glare. It paws the ground and moves forward, gaining momentum as it goes. The vibrations come through my feet until I feel them deep in my bones. Bending my knees, I wait for it. Red fog rises and falls and as it does images of the past flit across my thoughts. Rage builds as I hear a long-gone command to fire. No. I'm in control. I am myself.

Swinging as it comes into range, I pour everything I have into this one strike. Twisting my body into it, planting my rear foot and letting the power flow through, I slam my fist into the side of its head.

Its jaw opens, its head moves to the side, and it cries out in pain, stopping in its tracks. No time to let up, I hit it again with my other fist. The rage, red and hot, claims me as I pound my fists into it over and over. Its head jerks from one side to the other as I hit it over and over again. Hissing my rage.

It snaps at me, pulling back. I uppercut the underside of its jaw forcing its beak closed with a sharp snap. Seeing red, I continue hitting it. White pain flashes through the red fog, and it doesn't matter. I'm in control. I am myself. It snaps its mouth, but I duck to avoid it. Blood streams out of its mouth, and I hit it again.

It swings its massive head, knocking me to the side. Stumbling, I struggle to remain upright, but it hits me again, and I'm knocked to the ground. The ground underneath me jumps as it stomps closer, bouncing me off of it. I roll onto my back in time to see its open maw coming down at me. There's no time to get out of the way. Roaring, I thrust my arm into its mouth and grab its tongue, jerking it towards me. Its jaw snaps shut on my arm. I scream in pain, unable to contain it. Tightening my grip on its tongue, I jerk as it tosses its head to one side, dragging me along the ground.

"Drosdan!" Sarah yells.

The creature turns towards the sound, dragging me along.

"NO!" I yell, pounding it with my free hand.

Blood is streaming down its ugly head and splattering

across my face. It chews on my arm like it's a tough piece of meat that it's worrying at. I can't stop, can't let it hurt Sarah.

My feet scrabbling against the hard ground trying to find purchase, I finally get them under me and rise. I'm pounding the cherepakh's eye over and over and it's finally swelling shut. It opens its mouth to change its grip on me, and I rip, pulling its tongue out. It howls in pain, head rearing back, exposing the soft flesh of its neck. Slamming my elbow into the point where its softer under-shell meets the neck, I follow it up with several blows to the neck.

It shudders then drops to the ground with a thud. Rage consumes me and I don't stop. My fists fly into the monster but the images won't stop.

"I AM MYSELF!" I scream, hitting it more.

The General giving the order is all I can see. People cowering, begging for their lives, but he gave the order to shoot. When I told him no, my men would not shoot these innocents, he smiled and said a word, then, as one, we turned. I fought it, but there was no stopping it, my body was no longer under my control. When he again ordered us to fire, I did. We all did.

"Drosdan, stop, please, stop!" Sarah's voice cuts through the storm raging inside of me.

She has to be safe. She is all that matters. No longer will I be controlled. I am myself, I am hers. She is all.

"Drosdan, you've won, it's dead," she says, pleading in her voice.

When I look at Sarah, water is running down her face. I stop. My hands are torn and bloody. The cherepakh is a mess below me, very dead. Sarah comes close, touches me.

Cold emptiness expands out from my stomach, sending chills through my limbs as I stare at my hands.

"I am myself," I say, barely daring to say the words out loud.

"Yes," she says. "You are."

Rising, I turn towards the village and it all clicks into place. This is where it happened. I was part of the atrocity that happened here. Sarah moves next to me, and when I look at her, I know I'm not worthy of her. I'm a monster. It's been hidden in the fog of the bijass, but now I remember. I don't deserve her.

"I'm taking you back," I say, mouth dry.

"What?" she asks, confusion in her eyes.

"I'm taking you back," I say. "You deserve better than this, better than me. We'll leave in the morning."

Before she can respond, I walk away. Words can't fix what I am or what I've done. I'll return her to the City before I go into the desert and exile myself.

15

SARAH

"*D*rosdan!" I yell at his retreating back.

Blood drips from his tail and hands, staining the sand as he passes, but he doesn't slow or turn. My chest aches watching him walk away, and tears form in the corners of my eyes. A hot breeze blows, but a shiver runs down my spine. I want to follow him, I should, but moving is too much effort. It's all falling apart.

Black despair crashes over me, like a wave knocking me off my feet. Falling and tumbling over under its onslaught, I'm lost. Looking down at the carcass of the monster that Drosdan killed, anger flashes white hot, driving back the darkness.

"Screw you," I growl. "It's not ending like this."

I kick, hitting its hard shell, and pain shoots from my foot up to my chest.

"Damn it," I curse, hopping on one foot.

Despair under control, I storm after Drosdan. No way am I letting this go. He's almost past the buildings and into the courtyard, so I run, trying to catch up to him.

"Wait!" I yell.

He looks over his shoulder, and I wave my arms like a crazy person. It gets his attention because he turns around, but he doesn't look. His eyes stare at the ground between us, his shoulders are slumped, and his tail lies still on the ground. My chest constricts and my heart almost stops, when I look at him. I've never seen him like this. Bursting into a run, I close the distance between us and throw my arms around him. Tears fall down my cheeks as I hug him tight then smother him with kisses. He stiffens, arms at his sides, but I don't stop.

"Oh, Drosdan," I whisper in his ear. "Come on, let's clean you up."

Taking his hand, I lead the way to our home. I stir the coals of our banked fire to life, place a tin pot over the small flames, and pour water into it to warm. Drosdan stares at the ground. He is silent. Pulling him by both of his hands, I get him to sit next to the fire. Digging around, I find some pieces of cloth, and dip them in the warm water. Carefully, I clean his hands, which are covered with small cuts. Their bleeding is mostly stopped, and none of the wounds there are serious. Once I'm done with those, I turn my attention to his tail.

The wounds are deep and severe. When I first touch it, he inhales sharply.

"Sorry," I say, leaning closer to inspect it. Dirt and chunks of sand fill the open wounds making it impossible for them to scab over properly, and opening him up to a high likelihood of infection. "This is going to hurt."

Biting my lower lip, I set to work. He hisses and his tail twitches out of my hand.

"It's fine! Let it be," he says, rising.

Putting a hand on his shoulder, I push him back down and he doesn't resist.

"Stay," I say.

He looks over his shoulder at me and meets my eyes for

the first time since he killed the monster. The pain in his eyes makes my heart break again. It's so deep and raw I can see it there. Zmaj don't cry, but I'm sure if he was genetically capable of it, he would. My own tears flow for him.

"Sarah, it's okay," he says, but even his voice is despondent. Defeated.

"Drosdan, what is it?" I ask, touching his strong jaw and trailing my fingertips down to his soft lips.

He shakes his head, opens his mouth to say something, and then snaps it shut.

"It's nothing," he says.

"No, it's not," I whisper, scooting around to sit in front of him. Leaning closer, I hold his face between my hands and stare into his eyes. "Talk to me. I am your treasure, and you are mine. Tell me."

His eyes widen, a small gesture, but definite surprise. He opens his mouth again, closes it tight, and his jaw tenses.

"No," he shakes his head, pulling back from my hands. "I can't."

"You can," I say, taking his face in my hands again. "You must. It is our fate."

He inhales deeply, closes his eyes, holds the breath, then slowly lets it out.

"You do not understand," he says, opening his eyes.

"Then help me," I say. "Talk to me. Yell at me, give it to me. I love you."

Those last three words slip out of my mouth and the world stops. I can't breathe, my heart isn't beating, the fire doesn't crackle. Nothing happens as I wait for... something. Drosdan's eyes are locked on mine. We hold our breath. Anticipation. Something moves in his eyes, a change, nothing I can point to specifically, but I feel as much as see the shift. My heartbeat starts with a shocking force, pushing blood and making me light-headed. Breath rushes into my lungs, and the world resumes its march through time.

"I'm sorry," he says, shaking his head.

"For what?" I ask. I take my hands from his face so I can hold his hands in mine, sitting cross legged in front of him.

"I've done… terrible things," he says. "I am unforgivable."

"No," I protest. "No, you're not."

"You do not know," he answers, his eyes dropping to the ground.

"Tell me," I encourage him. He doesn't look up and doesn't resume speaking. We sit in silence that stretches out longer and longer.

"Drosdan, trust me," I beg him. "Please, trust me. We'll work through it."

He raises his eyes to meet mine, and I see him swallow then he sighs.

"You deserve the truth," he says. "You are right. When I return you to your kind, I want you to know, so you will not try to follow me. This is for the best."

"I'm not leaving you," I say. He doesn't answer, meeting my words with a stare. "I'm serious."

"We'll see," he says, sighing.

"Right, so tell me," I say.

His eyes focus beyond me, looking into the past. The fire crackles besides us, and a soft breeze blows whistling through the cracks in the window covers. I wait, letting him do this in his own way.

"Before the devastation I was a soldier," he says. "It was, of course, much different then. Some of the others think life was wonderful before the devastation, but they're wrong. Their memories are lost to the bijass, as were mine. In truth, Tajss wasn't much nicer then than it is now. The planet has always been deadly. The technology we had then helped, but the society was not necessarily good.

There was a lot of unrest. Some of them probably don't remember it, or maybe they didn't see it. As a soldier, I was on the front lines of it. When some village would rebel, my unit was deployed to quell the problem."

"They were rebelling? Against what?" I ask.

"The government, the Alliance, the off-worlders," he answers.

"Oh," I say, but not sure I really understand.

It's hard to imagine Tajss being populated or having a government, and especially hard to imagine off-worlders. It shouldn't surprise me, after Rosalind and Visidion were captured and spent time off-world. She said there is an entire galaxy out there, and somehow Tajss is believed devoid of life which is the only thing keeping it safe. Apparently at some point it was the center of a galactic civil war, which resulted in the Devastation, as the Zmaj call it.

"Especially the off-worlders," he says. "They ran the government, not openly but everyone knew it. The army was their tool. I didn't believe it, not until…"

He trails off, and I squeeze his hands to encourage him, willing strength into him. Whatever he is facing is hard and painful.

"Go on," I say and he inhales deep.

"We were dispatched to another uprising," he says, shaking his head, his tail twitching in irritation. "Routine. Shouldn't have been anything, but when we arrived…"

He closes his eyes, bows his head, then opens them and meets mine.

"You will never be able to forgive me," he says. "I cannot forgive myself."

"Try me," I say, squeezing his hands tight again.

A smile twitches at the corners of his lips, but can't overcome the weight of his sorrow. Rising into him, I kiss him gently, pouring courage and all my love into that point of contact between us. He doesn't respond at first, but I take his head in my hands and hold him close until his lips move against mine, and there is a proper kiss.

As I break the kiss and return to sitting in front of him, the air between us isn't as heavy. Satisfied, I smile and take his hands again.

"We came here," he says, the words falling heavy. "That's how I knew this place, I didn't remember it consciously, but buried in my memories, I did. This was a small mining village. A blip on the radar, nothing special in the grand scheme of things, but the miners were refusing to work. The conditions were deteriorating.

"The galactic civil war was raging, supplies to Tajss were running short. The heart of the war was control of Tajss, and that meant that the opposing forces were not only killing each other, they were raiding the trade lanes. Supply ships were being commandeered. So the miners here said they wouldn't work anymore. We were dispatched to handle it."

He shakes his head, jaw tightening.

"It's fine," I say. "Go on."

"When we arrived," he says. "They weren't armed rebels, they were families. Children, women, a handful of men armed with mining tools. No guns, no threat, only men who were trying to care for their families. They stood together, facing off against our well-armed platoon. The commander tried to negotiate with them, but they refused. Their children were starving, they needed food. Once supplies arrived, they'd go back to work. The commander turned to the off-worlder who was really running the show. A tall, thin yellow-skinned alien with saggy skin. When he opened his mouth, it would show rows of sharp teeth. The commander told the off-worlder that we should get supplies for them. It was a simple request. A reasonable one. How could we refuse?"

He stops speaking, swallowing hard. A distant scene plays in his memory as he struggles to find the words to express it to me. I wait, silent, holding his hands, and letting him work through it while giving him my support.

"The off-worlder gave the order," he says at last. "I refused. I turned to face him and told him no. We would not take action against these families. He smiled. A broad, evil smile, showing all those rows of sharp teeth. You will, he said. No, I answered him. Neither I, nor the men with me, would do this. It was wrong. He laughed and I got pissed. I brought my weapon to bear on him, fully intending to end him right there. I knew what it would mean for me, but I didn't care. I had to stop this madness.

"The off-worlder laughed again, looking down the barrel of my weapon. He met my eyes, grinning, and issued the order. Kill them, he said, and there was a weird echo of his words that reverberated over and over through my mind. My body turned, I couldn't stop it. I fought it with every fiber of my being, but I couldn't. The gun came to bear, but I couldn't stop seeing that yellow monster's grin.

"My finger tightened on the trigger and-"

He cuts off, mouth slamming shut as if he's biting off the words and stopping them from escaping into the world.

"It's okay," I say.

"No, it's not," he says. "I'm a monster. All my strength, I couldn't stop. His words kept echoing through my mind, and I obeyed, like some kind of automaton. All of us did. The moment we did it, the first of the bombs went off. As if in response to the atrocity we had done. The flash of it blinded me, and when I could see again, the bombs were falling everywhere. My unit was dispersed, it was over, but not before, not in time to stop what happened."

"Drosdan, it's not your fault," I say.

"It was and is. How could I not have stopped him? How

could I have done that?" he raises his hands between us. "How could these hands betray me?"

"I don't know," I say. "I do know that you're not that kind of man. I know you. Something doesn't add up there, and we'll figure it out."

"You are too kind," he says. "But it's settled. I will take you back to the others, then I'm going into the desert to find my fate."

"No!" I yell, grabbing his head and forcing him to meet my eyes. "No you will not. That would be the coward's way out, and you're anything but a coward. Something happened, a really long time ago, but yes, it happened. We'll figure it out, but I will not lose you to this or anything else! You're mine! You can't leave me, not like this, not ever."

"Sarah—" he says, but I cut him off by throwing myself against him and driving my tongue into his mouth.

He stiffens, pulling back, but I grab his head and force him to stay with me. My mouth moving against the hard line of his, until his lips soften, and he returns the kiss. Our lips move against each other, and I push my tongue deeper into his mouth, seeking and finding his. My hands run through his hair, pressing my body against him, my hard nipples overly sensitive to the rough cloth of my shirt.

His bulging arms wrap around, pressing me harder still to him. Moaning into his mouth, I grind my hips. His immense erection rises between us as he leans back until he's on his back. I move forward so that his massive cock presses hard against my clit. The pulsing sensation increases as my core tightens.

His hands run up and down my back, trailing along my sides, then up into my hair, pulling me down to him. Kissing as his hands run through my hair, I circle my hips, moaning as the tightness grows. Shoving one hand between us, I find the tie to his pants and loosen it, slipping my hand under the cloth. His cock jumps as I grab it, eager for my touch, and he groans in response. One hand goes to my ass, squeezing hard. Working my way out of my own clothes until I'm naked and sliding onto his shaft.

His half-lidded eyes stare up at me, his mouth a hard line, brow furrowed in concentration as I lower myself onto him. His incredible girth stretching, filling my pussy with its size. Wetness slips out, welcoming him in, and I take him fully in. His hands find my tits, massaging them as his cock finds the bottom. Closing my eyes and throwing my head back, I rotate in a circle.

He thrusts his hips up, forcing me up with him, then he retreats, an emptiness left behind as he pulls out. Before he's fully out of me, he thrusts up, burying himself to the hilt inside of me. Crying out in surprise and pleasure as he fills me. Instinct and desire overwhelm everything. Our bodies in motion to each other as we join, retreat and join again.

Pushing in and out, filling and retreating, building until my core becomes tighter than any coiled spring. Panting I try to hold it back, wrestling on the edge until I fall over into the sweet release of my orgasm. Drosdan cries out, and I feel his seed release into me, pumping into me forcefully. Every muscle tightens, my back arches, and stars dance across my vision as I'm rocked by the shock waves of the orgasm, leaving me breathless.

Slowly awareness returns, and I'm staring into his eyes, hands on his chest.

"Sarah," he says. "I love you, but I have to let you—"

"Shush," I say, placing a finger on his lips. "No talk."

He shakes his head beneath my finger, but I shake my head and shush him again.

"Listen," I demand. "What happened then isn't your fault."

"Yes, it was," he says. "I should have been able to stop it."

"How?" I ask, leaning over and kissing his lips.

"I don't know," he admits. "It was as if I was no longer in control of my body. I tried to stop."

"Yes," I agree. "You tried. You couldn't. There's more to this than we know right now, but here's what I do know. You're a good man."

"No, I'm a monster," he disagrees.

"Shush," I say, finger on his mouth again. "Don't say that again. You're not. I know you. I know you better than I've ever known anyone. I know your heart. I know your soul. You are my man, and you're no monster. I don't know what happened then, but it doesn't matter. We'll figure it out. What matters is this, you and me. Now. This moment. You are a good man. If you weren't, then none of what happened would bother you."

He nods under my finger, and I move it to kiss him.

"I love you," he whispers between kisses.

"You can never leave me," I say, throat tight.

"Never," he responds, arms tightening. "You are my treasure."

16

DROSDAN

"I don't like it," I say.

"I know," Sarah says, taking my hand in hers and gripping tight.

Staring down at the wreckage of the humans' ship makes anger churn in my stomach. They hate me, all of the Zmaj. These are the dregs of the human society. Sarah says they're scared, and every instinct I have wants to give them something to be truly scared of. The towering monolith of the generation ships wreckage casts a long shadow. There is a barrier constructed of crates and other odds and ends set in a wide circle around the wreck. It's an attempt at least to keep out the various predators that roam across Tajss. When I was last here there were armed guards patrolling the barrier.

"Where are the guards?" I ask, voicing my thought.

"I don't know," she says. "This isn't good."

Sarah bites her lower lip and shakes her head. Frowning, she squints against the low hangings suns, staring down at the ship.

"Maybe they went back," I suggest.

"No," she sighs. "I don't think so."

Something moves, emerging from the shadow of the ship's interior, pushing past the flapping plastic sheets hung across the opening.

"There," I point.

Sarah shields her eyes with her hands and gasps when she sees it herself.

"Tessa," she exclaims. "She looks terrible."

The female does look bad. Her skin is tight on her bones and has a dull gray hue to it, in sharp contrast to the healthy color of normal human skin. She appears to be nothing more than a pile of bones that is moving somehow. She stumbles forward until she reaches the barrier wall of crates. We watch as she opens one of them and pulls out a package. She turns around and heads back to the ship, but then two men emerge. These two appear much healthier and are carrying guns. We're too far away to hear their words, but they're not necessary.

One of the men raises his gun and aims it at Tessa. His mouth moves while the other one marches forward and takes hold of the package Tessa has retrieved. She resists, trying to hold on to it, but the man rips it away from her. As he does, she stumbles and falls. The two men turn their backs on her and reenter the ship.

"No, god damn it, no," Sarah hisses. Tessa doesn't rise. She's rocking herself slowly, holding her head in her hands. "Drosdan, wait!"

Her voice cuts through the rage, but the storm is vying for control. Looking over my shoulder, only now realizing I'm heading towards the ship. No male will treat a female that way. Not while I have breath.

"They have to pay," I hiss.

"Wait, we can't... not like this. It's dangerous," she pleads.

"Yes," I growl.

Red rage tears at my thoughts, instinct screaming for

domination. Those males will submit, the female needs protection. My tail rises behind me, stiff, hands clench into fists as my wings rustle.

"No, we have to be smart, careful. They're armed."

"I don't care, they're going to pay."

She runs closer, hands on my chest then on my face, pulling me down to meet her eyes. Her sweet, beautiful eyes boring into me, cutting through the swirling red fog of the bijass. A rock I can cling to against the primal instincts urging me to action.

"Drosdan, yes," she says, "but smart. We have to be smart. Let me go, alone."

"NO!" I shout, grabbing her arms and shaking my head. "No, you will not go there alone. I let you go before, never, never again."

She doesn't flinch, bending her wrists she grabs onto mine, rising onto her toes she kisses me. Her tongue forces its way past my stiff lips as her mouth moves against mine. The bijass, all the noise in my head stops. There is nothing but her, her lips on mine, her hands moving up my arms, across my chest. My primary cock stiffens as desire overrides all other instincts. Dropping her wrists, I grab her ass and pull her tight. Her body molds against mine as our tongues dance together.

"Listen," she whispers, pulling back just far enough to look into my eyes. "They'll shoot you on sight. Let me slip in, find out what's going on."

"No," I shake my head. "It's too dangerous. I can't let you."

Thoughts of those monsters harming her consume me.

"Trust me, I'll be fine," she says. "I'll tell them I escaped from you. They'll believe it. They think you're a monster anyway. It's what they want to believe. That all the Zmaj only want their women. You can sneak in close and do that thing where you hide in the sand. You'll be close if I need you that way. Let me at least try."

"If they harm you…"

She cuts me off with her lips. Her hand drifts down to my pulsating cock crushed between us. She slides her hand into my pants and grips it, stroking lightly while her tongue explores my mouth.

"I know," she says, gasping air then resuming the kiss.

"I love you," I break the kiss to say. "You are my treasure."

"And you are mine," she replies.

Sliding her hand out of my pants she takes a step back, placing both her hands on my chest.

"I don't like this," I say.

"I know, but it's the only way," she says. "If you go down there, they'll shoot on sight, no questions asked."

"I can handle them," I say, squaring my shoulders.

"Yes, I know, but how many people would be hurt in the process? What if they manage to hit you? We have to be smarter than this, Drosdan. Some situations take more than muscle."

My cock and anger pulse in time with each other. Turning back towards the ship, I force the red tide down and consider what she said. The anger, rage, base instincts have been how I've survived for as long as I can remember. The Edicts of the Tribe are the only control I've ever needed, often more than I've wanted. They don't allow for a female. There haven't been females among us since the devastation. There something deeper about a female, she touches something so deeply buried, so long gone it's not even a memory.

It's new. Different.

She's right.

I have to let her be headstrong, I can't control her. I can only love her.

I touch her face and trail my fingers down her jaw. Her

lips curl up into a perfect smile. Losing myself in her eyes, I know what I have to do. Cold fear creeps in, trying to find purchase, but I know what I must do.

"Okay," I say.

Inside it feels as if something breaks. I give up control, and no matter I know it's the right thing to do, it hurts. Her eyes widen, her hand cups my face, and moisture forms in the corner of her eyes. Her mouth opens, but no words come out, and she snaps it shut. Nodding she wraps her arms around me and I hold her, locking onto this moment, willing it to stretch into eternity, for in the next, everything will be different.

When she loosens her arms around me, the sensation of falling apart hits me, assailing my certainty, but I know this is what I must do. Letting her go, only so that I may truly have her. The suns are just over the horizon as we turn, holding hands, and look down on the ship. No one is outside that we can see from here. It's the perfect time to move closer. Inhaling deeply, I push aside the fears, concerns, worries, and the anger that lies beneath all of it.

"We've got this," she says with a heavy exhale, gripping my hand tightly.

"Right," I say, pushing down doubt and fear.

I am in control, I am myself.

She inhales deeply, squeezes my hand again, and then takes her first step forward.

"You'll be close?" she asks over her shoulder.

"Always," I say.

She takes her next step, then the next. Each one is a stabbing pain deep into my chest. Primal instinct screams at me to stop this madness. I'm sending her into danger, alone, and it goes against every fiber of who I am. She glances back once more, eyes locking with mine, uncertainty in her gaze. Nodding, I give her all the encouragement I can. She nods too, then she turns back towards the ship, stands straighter and walks forward, alone.

When she reaches the bottom of the dune, I move myself, heading to the right. Once I'm out of the line of sight of the opening into the ship, I move towards it, hunched over to make a low profile in case anyone does happen to look. I'm able to move faster than Sarah, so I should be in place before she arrives.

They've ringed the ship with a makeshift barrier of crates and pieces of metal. In minutes, I reach that without an alarm being raised and lie down on the loose sand. In a crawl, I move back towards where the opening is. I strain my ears to pick up any sounds of motion from the other side. The sound of a human crying drifts out of the ripped-open ship, a sad wail of despair. It's the only sound I hear. As I crawl forward, I spot Sarah approaching. Maneuvering my way to a position where I have a view of the opening through their makeshift wall and can still see Sarah, I bury myself in the sand and wait.

Dusk and shadows stretch across the sand by the time she is close to the wall.

"Hey! Hold it!" someone yells out of the shadows of the ship itself.

Two figures emerge, armed, probably the same men from before.

"Hey!" Sarah cries out, holding her arms up over her head. "Don't shoot!"

The two men approach, guns at the ready. My hearts pound in my chest, and every muscle tenses as they approach her. It will take me thirty seconds to close the distance between us. Thirty long, impossible seconds.

"Hey, you were kidnapped, what are you doing here?" one of them ask.

"I escaped," Sarah lies, arms still over her head.

"Right," the speaker says. "You don't look like a prisoner."

"I wasn't, he wanted me for…" she trails off, looking at the ground.

The two men look at each other, and one of them grins broadly.

"Oh yeah? Well, did you? Not sure we're going to want used goods here," he says.

My vision turns red as anger rages through me.

Breathe, I am myself, I think, struggling to control myself.

"What's happened here?" Sarah asks. "Where are the others? How come no one is out here working?"

"We're asking questions, not you," one of them says, motioning with his gun. "So answer us, did you?"

"Did I what?"

Too far. I'm too far away. I crawl forward, moving slow so as not to attract attention. Buy time Sarah, keep them talking.

"No!" she exclaims. "I would never, ugh, I couldn't let that… monster touch me."

Ignore her words, she's playing a role. Get closer.

"How did you escape?" the same man asks.

"Where is Tessa? Caleb? Jackson?" Sarah asks. "How bad has it gotten? Where's Gershom?"

The two of them exchange another cryptic look. The one who has spoken the most shakes his head when the other shrugs.

"What's happening?" Sarah asks.

"Nothing," the main speaker says, raising his gun to be level with her head. "You need to answer our questions."

"Sarah?" a female voice from inside the ship. "Oh my god, Sarah?"

The female we saw earlier, Tessa, emerges. She's skeletal and obviously not well, in sharp contrast to the two men interrogating Sarah.

"Tessa?" Sarah asks pushing past the two men.

"No!" the one who's been speaking yells, swinging his gun around and driving the butt of it into Sarah's stomach.

She yells, doubling over in surprise and pain. The rage claims me.

17

SARAH

*S*tars dance in front of my eyes as air whooshes out of me, and I double over, covering my stomach. Gasping, I try to pull in air, but nothing works. Gray edges my vision, tears well in my eyes, but air won't come.

Yelling, loud, can't make sense of it. Vision blurs, lungs scream, burning. Must inhale. Air. Must have air.

Head spinning, darkness closes in, going out. Fight it. Stay here, can't pass out.

One of them pushes me, and I try to straighten but my muscles are locked, not responding.

"Answer us!"

Suddenly there's a release, and air rushes in, bringing welcome relief. Chest burning, wiping tears from my eyes, gasping gratefully, I shake my head, trying to compose myself.

"Oh shit!" one of them exclaims, then he disappears out of the corner of my vision, screaming.

Shots fire, and I drop to the ground out of instinct, crawling across the loose sand. Something roars, a deep, guttural sound, accented by the staccato of rapid-fire electric bolts from a gun. Cold races down my spine, every nerve alight as adrenaline dumps into my body. Have to get clear. Shit, why isn't Drosdan here? Where is he? I know he's close, I need him. This is bad!

Sand gets in my eyes and up my nose. Sputtering, I keep moving. There is more screaming behind me and another roar. Something has breached the barrier. It could be one of a dozen or more monsters that call Tajss home. I should look. I can't. Look—no, escape.

The ship is close. Tattered plastic sheets flutter in the hot breeze. Close. Almost there. A sense of the familiar that somehow feels like it will be safe. It doesn't matter that it's an open wreck with nothing to stop the monster behind me. It's home, or was.

Clawing forward, I reach the edge of the plastic. Only now do I glance over my shoulder. Gunfire roars, bright flashes of light in the dusk making it hard to see, I can't tell what the monster is. Heart pounding in my throat, I gasp, cold freezing my veins. It's huge. It grabs one of the men, lifting him over its head, and throws. He screams as he flies through the air past the makeshift wall. The other man struggles to his knees. I'm blinking fast, trying to see as he brings his gun up and fires.

Rapid shots, buzzing electrical bolts cut through the air and slam into the back of the shadow. Its body reacts, jerking with each hit, but it doesn't drop.

That should have dropped anything, but not this. It roars and limbs spread wide as it turns.

My vision clears. What can't be happening is happening.

"DROSDAN!" I scream his name.

He doesn't look. His wings spread, his knees bend, and he leaps into the air, gliding towards the remaining guard.

The guard continues firing, but is shooting wild and missing. His eyes are wide, and he's blubbering like a baby.

Drosdan lands in front of him, sand exploding up, blocking my view for an instant. The guard rises into the air. Drosdan has him by the front of his shirt, holding him inches from his face.

"MINE!" Drosdan bellows.

The guard makes a fist, pulling it back, but before he swings, Drosdan tosses him. A casual flick of his wrist, and the man flies through the air past the barrier and lands outside it in a hump.

Drosdan throws his arms wide, tail standing straight upright, and wings spread, he hisses loudly, turning a slow circle.

No one and no thing challenges him. He hisses once more, then his body relaxes.

Every breath I take is a sharp stabbing pain. As the adrenaline runs out, awareness of it comes. It's not as bad if I breathe shallowly. Moving slowly, I get to my knees, then stop to breathe.

"Sarah," Drosdan calls.

"Yeah," I reply, gasping at the end as a sharp pain hits me.

Before my vision clears, I'm in his arms. He lifts me up, cradling me against his overly-muscled beautiful pecs.

"You're hurt," he says.

"It's fine," I whisper.

Tears run down my face, but not only from pain. Relief. He has me. The fear is gone. I'm safe.

Touching his face, trailing my fingers along his cheek, a light dances in his eyes, then he kisses me. Giving myself over to the kiss, all the pain fades before it.

"Shouldn't have let you go alone," he says.

"It's fine," I say. "I'm okay."

He squeezes, and I gasp.

"You are hurt," he says.

"Yeah," I agree. "I don't think it's... too bad."

The stabbing pain is worse. I can't take a deep breath—it hurts too much. Nice, shallow breaths, those are okay. Focus on that.

Gently he sets me onto my feet then kneels in front of me.

"Even on your knees, you're almost eye-level with me."

I can't stop the laugh, or the gasp of pain that follows it.

"Be still," he orders.

Starting at my neck, he runs his hands across my shoulders and down my arms then back up. As he passes my armpits onto my sides, I cry out when he reaches my ribcage. Slowly he lifts my shirt up. My right side is a dark purple from the middle of my chest around as far as I can see. His hands on my waist, he turns me to the side, inspecting the bruise.

"It's just a bruise," I say.

He glances up, his lips a hard line, then shakes his head.

Rising to his feet, he looks off into the distance. Not towards our new home, but towards the City.

"No," I say, shaking my head. "We can't, we have to save them."

"They don't matter," he says. "You need care."

"It's not that bad," I say.

"Sarah?" Tessa's voice comes from behind me.

Holding my side, I turn around to see her emerging from the wreckage. Several others come with her. All of them look terrible, well on their way to starvation. Skeletally thin and weak, skin bright red and blistered.

"Oh, god," I whisper, pain shooting through my chest, not from my wound.

"You've come back," Tessa smiles, then she's sobbing without tears.

"It's one of them," someone says from behind her, pointing at Drosdan.

"He's come to finish us," another voice whispers. "Where are the guards?"

The crowd of survivors talk over each other, espousing their wild theories.

Drosdan and I look at each other. He frowns and shakes his head.

"Help us," Tessa says. "Please, help us."

Silence falls over the dozens of survivors at her words. The sight of them is heart-wrenching. Gershom's experiment is a failure. They won't last another week without us. Meeting each of their eyes, there is a gamut of emotions, but mostly I see resignation. They've given up. There is nothing left to hope for.

Forcing a smile on my face, I reach out and take Drosdan's hand.

"Survivors," I say, raising my voice to be heard. "I can see how hard the past few weeks have been for you. I don't know what's happened here since I left, but it doesn't matter. You followed Gershom into the desert. It should be obvious to everyone here where that has left you.

"So I bring you a choice.

"Will you follow a Zmaj into the desert? We've found a place you can call your own. A small village, abandoned, it needs repairs, yes, but there is water and there is food. The choice is yours. Do you continue to follow Gershom's mad vision, or will you choose a new path?"

"He's just going to lead us to our doom," a male says.

"We've already found our doom," a woman responds.

They argue amongst themselves. Tessa comes over while they debate to stand with Drosdan and me.

"Are you okay?" she asks, glancing at Drosdan.

"Yes, I am," I tell her, smiling.

"He's not… making you?" she asks, hesitant.

Shaking my head, I chuckle and instantly regret it,

wincing at the stab in my chest. Closing my eyes, I breathe through the pain with short, shallow breaths.

"No," I say, opening my eyes once it's passed. "Believe me, he's not. If anything, I'm making him be here."

"Oh," she says, looking between the two of us. She meets Drosdan's eyes, frowns, then shrugs. "I'm sorry."

Drosdan tilts his head to one side, arching an eyebrow.

"Why?" he asks.

"I don't know what to believe anymore," she sighs then her body shakes with dry sobs.

Dropping Drosdan's hand I take her in my arms and hold her, ignoring the screaming pain in my side. Tessa breaks down, crying silently without tears.

"It's fine," I say, stroking her brittle hair. "Everything will be fine."

Drosdan shifts, uncomfortably looking around, obviously feeling out of place.

"I'm... sorry... so... sorry," she says.

"Drosdan, they need food. Can you go get something for them?"

Relief and concern mix on his face. He looks the crowd over with a critical eye, frowning.

"No," he answers at last. "This isn't safe."

"Get me a gun," I answer, nodding out towards where he threw the guards.

His frown deepens, but he leaves without another word.

I hold Tessa until she's cried out, and she straightens. As she does her hand grazes my right side, and I gasp in pain.

"Oh, Sarah," she exclaims, dropping to her knees in front of me. She lifts my shirt without ceremony or apparent concern for all the eyes on us. "You're hurt!"

"It's fine," I say, but cry out in pain when she touches the area without warning.

"Sarah!" Drosdan yells, and I hear his feet pounding the sound.

"It's fine," I shout. "Tessa is looking at the bruise."

His feet stop pounding on sand which is good. Tessa continues looking my bruise over, touching it with a much lighter touch now that is a somewhat less debilitating pain.

"You've got cracked ribs," she says. "This is bad Sarah. You need medical attention."

"So do you," I counter. Biting her lower lip, she doesn't argue.

"Food and water, we'll recover. That won't help this."

It doesn't matter that she's right. I can't leave these people here.

"Can you wrap them up? Are there any bandages left out here?" I ask.

"Yes, but that's temporary. You might have a pierced lung or internal bleeding. Sarah, I'm serious—this is really bad. You need to get back to the City. You need a doctor, medical machines. We don't have anything out here."

"I'll be fine," I say. "Get the bandages."

Drosdan comes back with both guns.

"Are there other guards?" he asks the crowd.

They exchange looks, fear on their faces. No one answers.

"Look," I say. "We're here to help. He'll go get food for you, but he's not leaving until he's sure I'm safe. If you want to eat, answer him."

"Food?" the murmur runs through them.

"No," a thin, balding man says. "Those two are the only ones left."

"Where's Gershom?" I ask. Silence falls like a heavy blanket. No one looks at us or each other even, finding something else to focus on. Drosdan hisses his frustration. "Well?"

"He's... gone," the balding man says at last.

"What happened? He was holding all the supplies for

himself when I left. How can he be gone when all of you have survived?" I ask.

"No one... knows... for sure," balding man says, holding something back.

"He was a liar," someone shouts from the back of the crowd but other voices hush him. "No, he was. A liar, and we all know it, even if we don't want to admit it."

"What do you mean?" I ask, searching out the one who is speaking in the crowd.

Silence greets my question stretching into another long pause. They shift their weight, quick glances, it takes me a bit to see it, but they're ashamed.

"Answer her," Drosdan hisses.

"He was taking epis!" the man from the back yells.

"We don't know that," balding man says. "It could have been... a disease or something."

"Are you saying he's...?" I can't even finish the thought.

It's a game changer. If Gershom is gone then why are they still here? Why didn't they return to the City when they figured out his betrayal?

"He's dead," someone answers.

"Then why are you still out here?" I ask.

"Why?" Balding man asks. "Why? Do you really have to ask? We're not welcome in the City. We don't want to live under alien rule. We don't want to watch them take our women from us. We don't want any of this! We just want to live in peace. Live our lives without them interfering."

Drosdan's tail drags across the sand making a swishing sound, and his wings rustle. The crowd looks at him with open fear. Tessa comes back out of the ship, bandages in her hands and stops, looking from the survivors to Drosdan and me.

"Okay," I say, a cold empty void opening in my core. Even now, facing certain death, they're blinded by their own hatred and fear. What would Rosalind do? That's the question. This group needs to survive. We need them if we're going to make it on this planet. Rosalind has run the numbers, and the gene pool of survivors is barely enough to prove viable past the next three generations. If we lose too many there will be inbreeding, and our entire race will die. "Drosdan get them some food, please."

"Sarah—"

"No," I cut him off. "I'll be fine, trust me."

He locks eyes with me, a silent battle of wills. His hands ball into fists, his jaw tightens, and he shakes his head. Butterflies dance in my stomach. I don't like facing off against him. Tension rises, the air becomes thick, and the crowd stares on with bated breath. I can't look away, can't flinch. I need him to do this. At last he hands me the guns and turns to go hunt. Tessa comes over, pulls my shirt up and reveals most of my breasts. Embarrassment floods me, knowing they're all watching. I stare at Tessa instead of looking up, pretending we're alone in a proper medical bay and not standing in front of crowd of hungry eyes.

"Hold this," Tessa says, putting my hand on my shirt.

Numbly, I obey. The bruise is worse, a lot worse. A purple so deep it's almost black covers my entire side. Damn it, I don't have time for this. Tessa places the gauze on my back behind the bruise, and sharp pain stabs, blinding me, and I gasp air until the stars clear.

"Sorry," Tessa says, gritting her teeth.

"It's fine," I lie.

She shakes her head and continues wrapping. As she pulls the bandage more tightly, the pain subsides to more manageable levels.

"There," Tessa says, tucking the ends of the bandage into itself.

"All right, you all have a choice," I say, dropping my shirt and looking at the crowd.

"You can follow a Zmaj into the desert and make a home for yourselves, or you can return to the City. The choice is yours, but staying here isn't an option. You're not going to make it."

"You can't tell us what to do," Balding guy says.

"No, I can't. What I can do is leave you here to die, which you are, or you can wake up, smell the non-existent coffee, and make your choice."

Balding guy opens his mouth to argue more, but either he realizes the truth in my words, or that it's futile, and his mouth snaps shut.

"You have to go to the City," Tessa whispers.

"I will, soon," I whisper back, watching the crowd.

Soon. I'm having a harder time breathing. The bandage is helping, but she's right. I'm going to need a doctor, but not yet. If I breathe shallowly and focus, I can keep the pain under control. For now.

Drosdan, Tessa, and I watch the assembled survivors. There's a soft murmur as they talk with each other. Anticipation is like ants crawling across my skin. Biting my lower lip I can only hope they'll make the right choice. They need to go back to the City. We need them there and I need medical attention I can only get there. Please, be smart. Get past your fear, please, please, please.

They turn into each other making a rough circle leaving Tessa and I standing outside. She and I glance at each other. She shrugs and smiles tentatively. It hurts too much to give her a smile back. Shallow breaths and the constant ache accented by moments of sharp stabbing hold most of my attention.

"Fine," bald guy says at last, the crowd turning around. As if that answers the question in anyway whatsoever.

"Fine?" I snap, anger flashing in response to his

provocation.

He grins. Stepping forward before I can stop myself, I'm going to slap that grin off his face. Tessa's hand on my arm stops me. I close my eyes and count to five, then open them and stare at the asshole who's provoking me. It's no wonder he followed Gershom into the desert, he's no better than Gershom was. Taking a breath, wincing at the pain, I let it out slowly.

"What is your decision?" I ask.

"We're going to follow the monster into the desert," bald guy says.

"He's not a monster!" I shout, anger flashing white-hot, but pain follows it, and I gasp.

"Right," baldy says. "Sure, anyway, that's our choice."

Shaking my head, I wipe away the tears of pain, grimacing.

"Fine," I say through gritted teeth. "Pack what you can carry. It's several days' journey."

"There's one more thing," he says.

Grinding my teeth, I struggle to control myself. Heat flashes across my skin, and my hand balls into an involuntary fist.

"Yes?" I growl.

"We keep the guns," he says. "Just in case."

That's a stupid idea. Stupid, stupid, stupid but can I win the argument? The options lay out before me, and I have to choose a path. If I refuse them the guns, they're not going to go. It will be a fight I can't win. If I give them the guns, then they have a very big advantage if they try to do something stupid. It's more than obvious they're stupid. They followed Gershom into the desert and even now, given the opportunity to go back to the comforts the City offers they choose to go further into the desert. They're not rational people.

"Fine," I sigh. "Start packing."

18

DROSDAN

*S*arah coughs, holding her side and grimacing.

"Are you okay?" I ask.

"Fine," she says between coughs. "It's fine."

She's lying to me. I feel it deep inside. She's hurt, badly.

"Can we take a break?" one of the other humans asks.

"No," I say, feeling no compassion. "We need to move faster."

"They can't keep up this pace," Sarah says.

"We don't have a choice," I say. "If we stay out here, we're at risk. This many people traveling is going to attract a zemlja. We need to get off the loose sand. The hard-packed sand close to the village means the zemlja aren't traveling there. Every moment we're out here our risk increases."

"I know," she sighs, shaking her head.

"So no breaks, not now," I say.

The survivors of Gershom's camp are strung out in a long line of stragglers. The food I brought them bolstered their strength but they're still weak. Weeks of minimum rations have taken a toll on them. It doesn't help that none of them are taking epis. Their bodies haven't adjusted. Of course if they had been, they'd probably be dead too, like Gershom.

"Why are you smiling?" Sarah asks.

"Hmm? Oh, nothing," I say, feeling the grin on my face get wider.

"Uh-huh," she says, staring at me.

"It's justice," I say, unable to resist her gaze.

"What is?" she asks, wrapping her arms around her chest, pain in her eyes.

"Gershom," I answer. "He got what he had coming."

"Yeah," she sighs. "Well, his influence is still being felt. Alive or dead, he changed the path of humanity forever."

The thrill disappears at her words. She's right. If not for him, these humans would be returning to the City. If not for him, it's doubtful they would have left in the first place.

"If we keep pushing, we'll make it by the end of the day," I say.

"Good," Sarah says, coughing.

Her cough sounds wet, rattling. She glances at the hand she covered her mouth with, then drops it to her side quickly, too quickly.

"How bad is it?" I ask.

"I'm fine," she says, wheezing.

My hearts increase, pounding in my chest. She needs to go back to the City. She needs help.

"They can make it the rest of the way on their own, let me take you to the City," I insist.

"We can't leave them," she says.

She's breathing shallowly. My scales itch, and a cold ball forms in my stomach. An urge to pick her up and run with her comes, and it takes all I've got to resist it. Gritting my teeth, I force my tail back down.

"Fine," I hiss, anger pounding.

"I know you're pissed," she says. "But we have to save them."

She's right. I know she's right, but it doesn't make this any easier. She is my treasure. The rest of them don't matter. Only she does.

Sarah coughs and makes a painful sound. My chest constricts and my hearts stop beating. This can't go on. I turn to her. Her eyes widen as I bend my knees.

"Drosdan… no," she protests, but I ignore her words and sweep her off her feet. "Put me down, I can walk."

"Of course you can, my love," I agree without complying.

She's stiff in my arms, resisting.

"Drosdan, I can walk. They all need help, I'm not going to be a giant weenie in front of all of them," she argues. "You're making me look weak."

"I don't agree," I say.

"Of course you don't," she says, slapping a hand against my chest. "You're big and strong, showing off all your… muscles."

"You're hurt. They're not," I say reasonably. "Besides, they could have their own Zmaj if they weren't all a bunch of jerks," I say.

Sarah snorts, laughs, then whimpers in pain.

"Don't make me laugh," she says, wiping moisture from her eyes as she relaxes in my arms at last.

"Sorry," I smile.

She rests her head against my chest, and before we've gone far, she's asleep. I listen to her breath, bringing up the rear and making sure that the stragglers don't get left behind. Each breath she takes wheezes, and her breath catches often. She has to be okay. She will be fine. I'll get her to the City, to a doctor, and they'll fix her. I keep pushing. We have to get there.

"Keep moving," I hiss at the stragglers.

They're too slow. Sarah's breathing seems to be shallower than it was. Every part of me wants to turn and run for the City. Leave these humans to fend for themselves. They made their choices, stupid as they were.

Drosdan, we have to save them. I hear her voice in my head.

The male I hissed at looks over his shoulder, eyes wide, face pale, and he straightens, moving faster. He's scared and that's good enough for me, if that's what it takes to keep him moving.

Fear teaches nothing, her voice whispers. It's real enough. I look down to see if she's awake. A whimper slips past her lips, and my hearts skip as cold fear washes through my limbs.

She has to be okay. Has to be. I can't face a world without her in it. While she consumes most of my attention, I can't help but notice the humans surreptitiously glancing at me. They're scared, sick, and no matter what, I think they are struggling. Struggling to survive, to understand, to come to terms with the world around them. Their fear is palpable, washing over me, amplifying the cold chills, pulsing through me. Of course they're scared. They followed a madman into the desert out of fear. Now they're being herded by one of the aliens they were trying to escape.

They're starving, exhausted, and without hope. Sarah stirs in my arms, whimpering as she moves, her breath hitching then evening out. Her face is pale and her lips have a blue tinge to them. My only hope is to get her back to the City. One hope, same as these humans I'm pushing towards the village Sarah and I found. One hope, hanging on by a thread. No matter if I hate it, I have to admit I'm scared.

A full grown zemlja, a rampaging herd of bivo, toe to toe with a guster, a threat I can face. Something I can hit. Anything but this. It feels like I'm spinning inside my own head as blackness swirls out of the gray fog of the bijass. Hopeless, no chance. I can't help her. Like them. A thin female with red-blond hair glances back, her lips a tight-hard line, eyes on Sarah. When she sees me looking at her she looks quickly away. Another tall male walks next to her, putting an arm around her when she stumbles, aiding her to stay upright.

"All of you!" I yell to be heard.

The humans stop in place turning toward me. A loose, rag-tag group of survivors that I haven't bothered to get a count of. It didn't matter as I was only doing this for Sarah. They gather together in a huddle, the males positioning the females behind them as if trying to protect them. From me. This is what they see. Fear.

Can I blame them? What cause have I given them to feel anything else? To expect anything but violence from me. Sarah stirs in my arms and her eyes flutter open. She meets my eyes, and a smile plays across her lips. She sighs, wincing as she inhales. She touches my face weakly, then her arm drops, and her eyes drift closed again. My stomach lurches and bile rises in my throat. The humans stare, silent, I can barely hear their breathing. The males shift from foot to foot, some of them holding makeshift weapons, trying to be ready for anything.

Looking at them, I don't have words. Words are Visidion's or Ragnar's, even. I've never been good with them. Sarah is good with them. None of them are here. I'm on my own. I have to make them understand. I have to get past their fear.

"We're not fast enough," I say.

"What?" the tall male who was helping the red-blond female exclaims, his voice rising and cracking. "We're doing all we can."

"No, we have to—"

"What in the hell do you expect of us?" he cuts me off, stepping ahead of the group.

He has a metal staff in his hand. It's thin and anything but dangerous, but judging by the way he grips it and holds it in front of himself, it must make him feel better.

"I understand but we have to—"

"Have to what?" he cuts me off again. My anger flashes, white-hot. "We're doing all we can. We're following your lead, towards what? How do we know you aren't leading us to our deaths?"

"I'm trying to save you," I hiss, struggling to contain my rage.

"Did you hurt Sarah? What's wrong with her?" he spits the words.

"Jackson—" the red-blond says, but not before I move.

Grabbing him by his shirt, I lift him one-handed into the air, holding Sarah in my other arm. The staff drops from his hand and clatters on the hard-packed sand. When I lower him to where his face is inches from mine, I can smell his sweat and fear. His mouth moves, but no sound comes out. The other humans gasp, accented by screams.

"Shut. Up," I hiss. "Listen."

After pushing him up into the air in a display of strength, I set him on his feet. I shift Sarah back into both of my arms before continuing.

"I know you're scared," I say to the group. "Sarah is hurt, but she won't let me take her to the City until you're safe. We have to work together, move faster. Males, each one of you, pair with a female. We're past the dunes and loose sand. We can reach our destination before the suns set."

They look at each other, silent, as if my words make no sense. I've worked hard to learn their language, did I use it wrong? The one who threatened me turns and faces them.

"He's right," he says. "We've come this far, so let's finish this."

He looks over his shoulder and I nod my head, encouraging him. The humans mutter, a swell of sound, then they begin nodding. The males pair off with females, and for the first time they move in something resembling a coordinated group. Sarah stirs, and looking down, she smiles.

"Good job," she says, her voice a soft whisper. She touches my cheek then her hand falls back. "Save them, please."

Pain stabs into my chest as her eyes close and a heavy sigh slips past her lips. The male who stood up to me watches the red-blond female next to him from a few feet away.

"Move," I hiss, voice hoarse as the sound travels out of my tight throat.

The male nods and turns to go, but the female moves towards me and he stops, watching her. She puts her hand on Sarah's face, wiping away beads of moisture.

"She has a fever," the female says, looking up at me.

"A… fever?" I ask, uncertain of the word or what it means.

She nods, frowning deeply.

"Jackson, she needs a doctor. A real one. He should take her to the City, now."

The male walks over.

"Tell me how we reach our goal," he says. "Can I get us there without your help?"

He meets my gaze with his jaw set and cold, hard determination in his eyes. Tajss is dangerous, always, but more so for these soft humans. I shouldn't leave them. Sarah wouldn't want me to. What if they run into guster? We're deep into the hard-packed sand, so a zemlja isn't likely. If zemlja traveled through here, the sand would be soft and rolling as it is across most of Tajss. I don't remember why this is, but I know there are areas, such as this, that they don't travel.

There's something to that I feel like I should remember, but it's lost in the fog of the bijass.

"I doubt it," I say.

The female looks up from Sarah staring into my eyes then looking at Jackson.

"We have to," she says.

"Right," he says, his shoulders slumping he drops his head to stare at the ground. He inhales a long, deep breath then straightens himself and meets my gaze.

"Sarah is a good girl," he says. "And apparently she sees something in you. What, I don't know, but that's not my problem. We owe her this. Tell me how to get to our destination without you."

Staring into Jackson's eyes I see determination and a resolve of steel. Beyond him, the rest of the humans huddle watching. My commitment to Sarah's desire wars with my need to save her. She is my treasure, making the war decidedly one-sided. I put a hand on his shoulder, and he flinches but doesn't pull back.

"Keep Estejan above your shoulder, like this," I say, turning him until he's positioned facing where I know he would intercept the village.

"Estejan?" he asks, confusion on his face.

"The primary sun, that one," I explain, pointing it out for him. "Keep it just over your shoulder. Like this, here."

"What about when it goes down?" he asks.

"You're in trouble," I say.

Biting his lip, he nods. "Okay, don't let that happen then."

"Right, you have to reach the village first. If you hold a steady pace, you'll make it fine."

"If we don't get eaten by some random-ass monster," he says.

"There is always that," I agree.

He looks at the female who is watching him with what I

can only define as admiration. Their eyes meet, and I feel the spark between them. He's doing this for her. He wants her to be his treasure. I squeeze his shoulder once and pat his back.

"Right," he says. "We should go and so should you."

"You can do this," I tell him, something in the way I see him changing.

He's not weak or stupid as I had assumed. In him, there is a leader waiting to be born. He goes and stands next to the female. When he turns around, a half-smile plays across his face.

"Hey," he says. "Anything happens to her, I'll kick your ass."

My tail straightens at his threat, but then I realize he's not serious. I've seen the other humans doing this, putting up a front of bravery when scared or uncertain. Letting my tail back down to the sand, I nod in respect to him and spin on my heel, shifting Sarah in my arms as I do.

"Run," the female says. "Run, Forrest, run!"

I have no idea what her words mean as a whole, but the command to run is exactly what I do.

19

DROSDAN

"OPEN THE GATE!" I yell.

Muscles ache, wings are screaming agony tearing through, and every breath hurts, but I don't slow. Sarah hasn't woken for hours. I've run through the previous night and all of this day. The suns are setting once more, but the wall is in sight and beyond it the caves of home. The gate has been finished since I left, and the wall is repaired and complete. Someone, I can't make out who, looks over the wall then drops out of sight. As the gate swings open, I dig deep into the last bits of reserve I have left.

The fire in my core flickers, but my love of her is all the fuel I need. Pushing with everything I've got, I run faster. I bend my knees and leap, angling my wings to catch the wind despite the pain. It's sharp, blinding, causing stars to dance across my vision. Close. Almost there. Push. Push. She'll be okay. The healer will save her.

Sand explodes around me as I land, run three steps, then leap again, closing the distance to the gate. Shadowy figures emerge from the opening. I can't make out who they are. Dim light, vision clouded by pain and exhaustion—it doesn't matter. Get her to the caves, to the healer. It's all that matters. They close around me, but I don't slow for them. Arms reach, but I knock them aside as I run through the opening.

"ORMARR!" I bellow, the healer's name tearing my dry throat. "ORMARR! HERE!"

Figures are all around, watching, coming towards me. I can't see clearly. My eyes are dry, filled with sand, and pain blurs everything. Where is he?

Someone jumps in front of me, blocking my path. I dodge to the left and they move with me, so I go right, but they continue blocking.

"Out of my way before I destroy you!" I hiss.

"Drosdan, stop, Ormarr's here," Ragnar says. "Give her to us, let us help."

"I'm here Drosdan, stop, let me see," Ormarr says.

His scales are bright, brighter than any other Zmaj I know. His brightness makes him stand out in the blurry vision. Cold chills run across my scales and a shudder races down my spine. Sarah is lifted from my arms, and the emptiness forms its own ache, competing against the soreness. Dropping my arms to my sides and losing myself in the noise of others. Rapid fire talking but the words don't make sense, they're sounds that have no meaning. Someone grips my shoulders, and numb, I'm guided away. In a flash it hits me that I'm leaving her.

"She can't be alone! I have to be with her!"

"Drosdan," Ragnar says, and he's holding on to me.

Ripping myself free of his grip, I spin as a fresh clarity comes through. My vision clears and I see Ormarr carrying Sarah towards the caves. My tail slams Ragnar as I move. He exclaims in pain, but I ignore him. Bending my knees, spreading my wings, I can close the distance with a single leap. As I spring, a weight lands on my shoulders, blocking me.

"Get off me!" I scream, stumbling forward, struggling against the weight on my shoulders.

Scrambling to get free, I grab a limb, twisting until there's a popping sound.

"Aggh," Ragnar cries out. "Bashir! Padraig!"

The others close with me, leaping into the fray. The bijass rises and the moment narrows. Simplicity. Fear fades in the face of an opponent. Me versus them. They want to keep me from my treasure. Hissing, dropping my shoulder and jerking the limb I'm gripping, Ragnar flies off of me. Padraig bellows, and his deep voice echoes, bouncing off the stone, the wall and the cliff of the caverns. A smile forms on my face as the red rage claims me.

"Drosdan," Bashir says, circling to my left. "Calm down. Remember the Edicts."

Edicts. What do they matter? Without her nothing matters. I don't matter.

Bashir moves in, grabbing most of my attention, but it's a feint, creating an opening for Padraig, who rushes in like a charging bivo. His massive arms spread wide, he embraces me from the side, lifting me off my feet, pinning my arms and wings. He's strong, but I'm stronger. My tail is free, so I slam him in the legs. Grunting in pain, he loosens his grip, only a little, but enough. Straining, I break his grip, dropping to the ground and bringing my right elbow up into his jaw. There's a satisfying crack as I connect and he stumbles back, blood flying from his mouth.

Tail straight up behind me, I roar a battle cry, putting my full attention on Bashir. Bashir shows no fear, a hardened warrior, he circles, looking for an opening. I turn with him, watching for others to join him from the sides.

"Drosdan, we're helping her, control yourself," Bashir says.

Words. Distant and without meaning. I hear them, but the

storm of the bijass, the rage and primal urges drown them. Ragnar is on his feet, closing. I feint at Ragnar, and as he steps back, Bashir moves to close, but I'm ready. Grabbing Bashir's arm, I wrap my arm around his, locking his elbow. Applying pressure, I force him to his knees. He grunts, suppressing the pain. Pointing at Ragnar, I motion for him to come closer.

"Try it, I'll destroy you," I hiss. "She is mine."

Ragnar holds up his hands, palms facing me, then turns them so that his palms are towards the sky, indicating his submission. His tail lowers to the ground and he closes his wings. Hissing, I increase the pressure on Bashir's arm, and he grunts louder. The elbow is close to breaking.

"She is," Ragnar says. "She's yours. No one is challenging you. We're helping her, Drosdan. Edicts. Remember the Edicts. Say them with me. I am—"

A blur of motion to my left grabs my attention. I spin towards it, but I'm too late. It hits me in the head with a high-pitched scream and stunning force. My head rings as I stumble backwards, losing my grip on Bashir's arm. Someone is wrapping themselves around my head and chest. Can't see. Blows rain down, hitting me anywhere they can. Roaring in rage, I scrabble with my opponent. Find a grip. Grab anything. He's slippery—every time I almost get a grip, he shifts and slides. Claws dig at me, sliding across my scales, and then something stabs into my right eye.

Roaring, I get a grip at last and throw my opponent off. Blind in one eye, I crouch, prepared for an attack from anywhere. Turning from one side to another. A circle has formed around me. Ragnar is in front, hands held out in submission. Bashir is to my side, his left arm hanging limp. Padraig pushes out of the circle and joins them, blood dripping from his nose and mouth. Pleasure rushes through me. Them against me, for her. Simple. Kill or be killed. She is all that matters. Spreading my wings, tail straight up, I throw my arms wide, roaring a challenge.

"Drosdan, stop this," a female steps in front of Ragnar out of the crowd.

A blonde halo of hair surrounds her head. She's heavy with child, her voice soft and soothing. It cuts through the rage to where I am, in the middle of the storming bijass. Huffing, chest out, I hiss. The bijass swelling, pushing to maintain control.

"It's enough," a dark-skinned female with high cheekbones steps out to stand next to the other female.

Delilah. Mei, the blonde is Mei. The rage feels hollow.

"Stop this right now," Olivia says, stepping up next to them, her red hair shifting in a soft breeze. She crosses her arms over her ample chest, tapping a foot.

The bijass falls away leaving me cold and empty. I drop my arms and tail, my shoulders slump, and my head is too heavy to hold up. Pain forms in my chest, making it hard to breathe. Shaking my head, I struggle to inhale. The females come closer, placing their hands on me, making soft, reassuring noises. The crowd around us disperses as they lead me towards a cavern. I'm following their guidance because I've no will of my own left.

I can't save her. There is nothing I can do.

Helplessness. A feeling I've never had before, but there is no other name to give it. Sarah is hurt, badly hurt, and there is nothing I can do. Sit here, wait. Helpless.

The females dab at me with wet cloths, applying salve. It's motion happening around me, but it means nothing to me. There is nothing I can do but wait. They bring in Padraig and Bashir to tend to their wounds. Ragnar carries Samil in as well, placing him on a cot covered with furs. My attention goes to Samil. He doesn't seem to be conscious.

"What?" I can't form more words, they slip away before I

can push them out.

"He's the one who attacked you," Mei says, wiping a cloth across my injured eye.

"Samil?" I ask, confused. "He's…"

She stops and gazes into my face, waiting for what I'm going to say, but it stops me.

"He's what?" she asks, waiting.

Head spinning, I can't think of what to say in response. Samil? Attacked me?

"Brave? Bold? Throwing himself against you? Knowing damn well he didn't stand a chance?" she asks, arching an eyebrow and tapping a foot.

I shake my head and say nothing. She resumes tending my wounds, but she's being rougher now. It's fine. A bit of pain is the least I deserve. It's focusing. Anything to keep my attention off of not knowing what's happening with Sarah.

"Is he hurt badly?" I ask.

Mei looks over her shoulder towards him.

"I don't think so," she says. "He hit his head when you threw him, knocked him out."

"Any word on her yet?" I ask.

"Ormarr is still with her," Mei says.

Ryuth pushes through the crowd outside the door followed by Olivia. Olivia has a baby in her arms drawing my eyes as it coos softly. Ryuth goes to Mei and places a protective hand on her swollen belly. Olivia goes to stand next to Ragnar who takes the baby from her, lifting it up over his head. The baby giggles as Ragnar swooshes it through the air, up and down, landing kisses on its face each time he brings it near his face. My stomach lurches watching him as it hits me I might never have it. It's an empty, black void, devoid of hope waiting. One wrong move, and I'll fall into it, losing myself forever. Ragnar makes soft sounds to his child, and a sad melancholy fills me.

"You owe me," Padraig says, his voice nasal, glaring.

Bailey, an older female with gray hair at the temples of her shoulder-length auburn hair and crow's feet at corners of her eyes walks into the room, interrupting my staring contest with Padraig when she comes to stand in front of me. Mei silently hands her the cloth she was tending my wounds with and steps aside.

"You've made one hell of a mess," Bailey mutters, leaning in to get a close look at my wounds.

"Where's Sarah?"

"She's with Ormarr," she answers.

"Why aren't you there too? You're a doc-tor," I stumble over the strange human word for a healer as I rise to my feet. "She needs you."

Bailey pushes me down with a surprising strength from her frail body. I could push past it of course, but doing it might hurt her. I've caused enough pain.

"He's doing a fine job," she says.

"How is she?" I ask, insistent.

Bailey straightens, meeting my pleading eyes, pursing her lips. I can see her thinking over her answer before she finally speaks.

"Bad," she says.

"No!" I cry, pain stabbing deep into my hearts and constricting my chest. It's overwhelming, more than I can contain. The pain has depths I didn't know I could feel, bottomless.

The males in the room tense, turning. Ragnar hands his child to Olivia in a single fluid motion as his tail rises. I hold up my hands flat, palms up in submission, I'll not lose myself, not again. Tension drains as if the entire room takes a collective breath at once. Bailey resumes dabbing at the cuts, and the murmur of conversation rises.

"It's bad but Ormarr is good," Bailey continues.

"She's human, why aren't you there too?" I ask, a pleading note in my voice I can't control. "What does he know of humans?"

She stops, desert storm clouds in her eyes, jaw tense, lips pursed tight staring into my eyes. "I've done all I can."

Closing my eyes my hearts pound in my ears. A dull roar drowning out all other sound. My chest aches, can't get enough air—my treasure.

"Drosdan," Bailey says, trying to push me down.

Ignoring her, I stand and walk out of the cave. Distantly they call my name, but it doesn't matter. I have to be with her. The suns stab into my eyes as I step onto the ledge and turn, but I am numb. I walk up to Ormarr's quarters. She has to be there.

People work in the garden. Laughter and soft voices drift along the breeze. None of it seems real. The world is a dull, washed-out gray. Sarah. My Sarah. If anything happens to you I'll...

No, she's fine. She'll be fine. She has to be okay.

When the opening to Ormarr's quarters is before me, I hesitate. Sounds of movement emerge along with his voice, ordering someone, confident and sure. My eyes adjust to the flickering light inside the cave slowly. At first there are only shadows, but my protective lenses open, allowing me to see clearly. Ormarr turns, his body blocking the bed behind him.

"Drosdan, you shouldn't be here," he says.

"I... have to be," I say, motioning with my useless hands, trying to see past him. "Is she..."

No. Don't say it. She's okay. She has to be. It can't end like this. Ormarr's eyes tighten, looking away from me, he inhales deeply. My stomach sinks, and cold chills run down my arms.

"No, it's fine," I say. "She's tough. I know she'll be okay. Just... how long do you think she needs... to recover? We should probably talk to Rosalind and Visidion. We'll need to go to the City—"

Ormarr shakes his head and meets, my eyes and I lose my thought.

"Drosdan," he says, placing a hand on my arm.

"She's fine," I insist.

"No," he says. "She's not. She's been hurt, badly. I've done all I can, but she's human. Bailey has tended to her as well, we've done all we can."

"You haven't," I say, my voice rising. I grab his arm and squeeze. Ormarr winces at my grip as I shake him. "What does she need? Name it. What do you need to help her?"

"We have to get her to Draconov. The machines there will let us see what's happening inside. It's our best chance."

"Fine, let's go," I say.

"Drosdan, you're exhausted, how long have you been up? How far did you travel across the desert carrying her?"

Cold certainty swells through me as I meet his eyes. Gripping both of his arms in mine I jerk him close lifting him off his feet, glaring.

"Get her ready," I hiss.

He meets my gaze for a moment before he drops his eyes and nods his agreement. I drop him to the ground, push past him, and kneel next to her.

She's pale. There's almost a gray color to her skin. Her hair is plastered to her face and head. She's breathing shallowly, but I don't hear the hitch in her breathing she had before. I brush the errant hairs from her face, lean in, and kiss her forehead.

"I love you," I whisper in her ear.

She sighs, or it seems she does. In that sigh, I hear her response. She loves me. She is my treasure. This is a test, and I will not fail. She is mine, and nothing will stand in my way. I will save her.

20

SARAH

*P*ain.

Blinding, white-hot pain.

My mind cringes back from it, and darkness comes and washes it away. It's too much to deal with, and I welcome oblivion as it takes the pain away.

Time passes. I don't know how much, or how I know it has, but it feels later. Awareness comes slowly. Pain is there. Pain, but not as much.

A scraping sound, then something cool touches me. The cool sensation moves across, tracing lines on... something, my body. Right, that's me. It's heavy. So heavy.

Eyes, open, come on. Damn they're so heavy. Aren't they supposed to do what I say?

There's a roaring sound. Ears. Right, it's in my ears, something pulsing, pounding like a dull rush. What is that?

Oh. Its blood, pushing through my body. Right. So I'm alive? Death can't hurt this much, right?

"Sarah?" Drosdan's voice comes from some unimaginable distance. The far side of the universe, perhaps. "Sarah, wake up."

His words are a golden trail cutting through the darkness. Latching on to them I follow, pushing through the heaviness, resisting the pull to sink back into the black. Focusing, following the trail of words, there's something lighter. Yes, there, follow it. Open eyes, damn you, open!

They do, and then bright light stabs in, and I close them in immediate regret.

"Sarah!" Drosdan exclaims.

Mouth is dry. So, so dry. Opening and closing my mouth, I try to work some moisture in. I can't answer him. Words won't form past my parched throat. Something wet and cool passes my cracked lips, sweet relief, quenching my thirst. Better, so much better. Okay, let's try the eyes again. When I open them, they're dry, but by blinking a lot, the hazy blur that passes for vision slowly comes to focus. Drosdan is hovering, inches from my face.

"Hi," I say, but it sounds more like a croak.

Swallowing hard, I force a smile. His scales are edged with a dull yellow-orange shade I've never seen on him. My hand doesn't want to obey at first, but by concentrating hard I lift it to his face, cupping his cheek before the effort becomes too much, and I let it drop back to the bed.

Bed. I'm on a bed. A real bed, not a make-shift thing like we had at the village or the piles of furs they use at the caves. There's a beeping sound too. Darting my eyes around because moving my head is entirely too much effort, I can tell there are machines around me. We're in the City.

Shit, Rosalind.

"It's fine," Drosdan says, brushing a hair away from my eyes as if he read my thought. "Trust me, it's okay."

"The City?" I ask, my throat is sore and talking is uncomfortable.

"Yes," he nods. "Ormarr and Bailey did all they could for you. I had to bring you here."

He has heavy, dark circles under his eyes. Poor Drosdan, an ache in my chest forms behind the overall pain my body is feeling.

"Oh," I say, letting my eyes drift close mostly of their own accord. I know the room isn't bright, especially by Tajss double-sun standards, but it's still hurting my eyes.

Drosdan's finger trace along my forehead, down my cheek, then back up and over again. He brings a cup up to my lips and tilts so a drop of water touches them. Drinking it, grateful for the sensation of sand being washed down my throat, easing and cleansing the dryness.

"Easy love," he says, voice soft. "A little at a time. Jolie says not to overdo it."

It's like the nectar of the gods, and I don't care what Jolie thinks, nothing has ever been sweeter than this. I gulp at it, straining to get more, until suddenly my stomach clenches tight and I'm spluttering as my body convulses. Coughing and choking. Drosdan hooks an arm behind me, lifting me up and tapping lightly on my back.

"Damn it," I mutter, regaining control. "Don't say it."

"You're fine," Drosdan lies, a smile playing across his lips.

"Liar," I say.

"He's not lying," Jolie says, appearing next to the bed as if summoned. "You're fine, not great, but you know, okay."

She smiles, laying a hand on my forehead then my cheeks. She turns and stares at a monitor next to the bed that has symbols dancing across it which make no sense—to me at least.

"How bad is it?" I ask.

Jolie glances over her shoulder before putting her attention back on the monitor. She and Drosdan exchange a look that doesn't feel like it bodes well.

"You're going to be fine," she says, not looking at me.

"Okay, then... what?" I ask.

"How's the pain?" Jolie asks.

"Tolerable," I say, taking a moment to assess. "My chest hurts, but I can breathe, and it no longer feels like something is stabbing me every time. Head hurts too."

Jolie nods as she turns back to me. She pulls back the blanket off my chest and lifts the gown I'm wearing. Only now do I see the wraps around my ribs and the bruise that stretches out from underneath it. It's an ugly dark purple edged with yellow. No wonder it hurts so much.

"All to be expected," Jolie says.

"Ouch!" I exclaim as she touches my side. "How about not doing that!"

"Sorry," she says. "You broke four ribs, and one of them was puncturing your lung. You're lucky to be alive."

"Damn," I say, grabbing Drosdan's hand and squeezing it.

What she really means is, I'd be dead if not for him. Drosdan smiles, squeezing my hand back.

"I'll need to monitor your progress, but it seems to be healing well," Jolie says. "So that's good."

"Yeah," I agree, staring into Drosdan's eyes.

Worry lies heavy on him. The air is thick with unspoken words. If nothing else, Rosalind has trained me well in reading a room. All the little signs, body language, feelings, looks, they tell a story. I've made my life out of reading them and trusting my gut. There's a whole lot not being said. It doesn't take any brilliant insight for me to guess what it is.

Rosalind and Visidion.

They can't be happy with Drosdan or me either. Facing their wrath isn't going to be fun. In the end we did what we had to do, but explaining that to Rosalind... she's reasonable. She'll get it.

Eventually.

First, we have to get past her anger. She will be right-eously pissed. I can't blame her, or I won't anyway.

"Oh, ow, uh," I mutter sighing. Deep breaths aren't a good idea it seems.

"Take it easy there, tiger," Jolie says, looking me in the eyes for what must be the first time.

"Right," I agree, wincing at the continuing pain.

"I can give you something for the pain," Jolie offers.

"No," I say. "It's fine, I'll push through it. How's Rverre?"

Jolie's face lights up so bright the suns could be shining into the room. Her smile is ear to ear, and she laughs.

"You won't believe how much she's growing! She's runs after Illadon determined to do whatever he does but better. He decided to climb up a dresser yesterday and leap from it to the bed, which is at least eight feet away. I walked into the room just in time to see him flying and her halfway up the dresser right behind him."

"Oh no! Was he okay?" I ask.

"He was fine, he's every bit as tough and strong as his father," she says, shaking her head. "And as fearless. I wish he would learn just a bit of fear. Nothing scares him and any idea he gets in his little head he acts on."

"Sounds like you and Calista have your hands full," I observe.

"Like you wouldn't believe," Jolie says. "It's okay though. We have lots of help. Everyone is always willing to babysit. I swear it's almost as if I have to book time with my own kid!"

I laugh and instantly regret it as pain stabs through my chest. Holding my side I push away the humor, smiling instead.

"Okay, no laughing," I say.

"You're going to hurt for a while," she says. "We've got the ribs back in place and they're fused together, but I can't speed up the healing of the bruising and trauma."

"It's fine, thank you," I say.

"Okay, well I should go," Jolie says.

"Thanks again," I say.

"I'm glad I could help," she says. "Calista and some of the others are wanting to check in on you, if you feel up to it?"

"Of course, I'd love to see them," I say. "Maybe after a nap though?"

Exhaustion lies heavy across my body. I've done nothing, but it feels like I've run a marathon.

"Sure," Jolie says, opening the door to leave. She stops and turns back around. "There's one more thing."

"Yeah?" I ask, anticipation sending cold tingles and making goosebumps on my arms.

"Rosalind wants to see you... first," she says.

"Yeah, I kind of figured," I say. "Whenever she wants."

Jolie nods and leaves, closing the door behind her.

"You should rest," Drosdan says.

He hooks a stool with his tail and it scrapes loudly as he drags it closer.

"How pissed is she?" I ask, closing my eyes.

"It will be okay," he says.

"So, really pissed," I reply.

"Rest my love, I am here with you," he says.

"I know, thank you," I say.

"You have nothing to thank me for," I say.

"I have you to thank for everything," I say. "Saving me, saving the survivors, we got them to the village, right?"

He doesn't answer me immediately so I open my eyes and look.

"We did, right? I remember... being close," I say, digging through the hazy memories of the last few days. Still, he doesn't answer, staring at the floor and not meeting my eyes. "Drosdan..."

"We did...," he trails off, staring at the floor.

"Drosdan?" I ask, sitting up the best I can.

"I left them half a day away," he says, hunching his

massive shoulders. "You were getting worse, there was no time."

"No," I whisper, unable to make a louder sound.

A cold hard ball sits in my stomach. He left them, starving and alone in the desert. This is exactly what I didn't want to happen. Damn it, it's my fault. If I hadn't mouthed off to the guard, he wouldn't have hit me. I didn't think things had gotten as bad as they had. If I'd known Gershom was dead, I would have been more cautious. Asshole or not, he did keep some modicum of control over the more radical of his followers.

How many of them survived? Are they infiltrated in with the other survivors? If not, where are they? Shit, this is exactly the kind of questions Rosalind is going to have, and I don't have any answers for her.

"I'm sure they're fine," he says. "We weren't far when I left them, and I had the male Jackson take the lead. The group agreed to follow his direction."

"You got that group to agree to follow Jackson?" I ask, arching an eyebrow.

"Yes," he says, glancing up and meeting my eyes, but only for a moment.

"Well that's impressive," I say. I collapse back onto the bed, letting out a breath I didn't realize I'd been holding.

"We can check on them, once you're feeling better," he says, taking my hand again.

"Yeah," I agree, closing my eyes and waiting for a wave of pain to pass. "First we'll have to talk to Rosalind and Visidion. I know they're pissed, how bad is it?"

"They'll get over it," Drosdan says.

"Yeah, I don't think it's going to be quite that easy," I say.

The door squeaks as it opens, and I look to see who's coming in. That falling feeling as if I'm falling through the bed comes over me as Rosalind enters. Mostly I wish I could sink through the bed, the floor, and be anywhere but in front of her. I'm not worried about her anger, anger I can handle. I'm worried that she's going to look at me in disappointment. That I don't know how to handle.

She steps in and Visidion comes in behind her. Rosalind is in her immaculate white space armor, of course, and her beautiful dark hair hangs perfectly down past her shoulders. The air she carries around her is one of total control. She dominates any room she walks into without a word. Her sharp eyes lock on mine, and I barely notice Visidion behind her. The Zmaj Commander is big and burly, but nothing compared to Drosdan. Still, he has the same ability to command a room, unless Rosalind is there. I've worked with both of them, and I know he chooses to give her control.

"How are you?" Rosalind asks, stopping next to the bed opposite Drosdan.

"Better, thank you," I say, wanting nothing more than to drop my eyes but unable to. She's locked onto me, and I'm frozen, mesmerized by her.

"Good," she says. "Do you mind?"

She motions at my chest, and almost imperceptibly I nod my agreement. She slides the blanket aside, lifts my gown up, and inspects the bandaging and bruising. She nods sharply as if satisfied then replaces the layers.

"You're very lucky," she says. "If Drosdan hadn't gotten you here when he did, we'd have lost you."

"Yeah," I say, at a loss for words. This isn't going anything like I expected.

Rosalind takes a step back from the bed, and I'm able to breathe easier. Anticipation is killing me. I'm waiting for her to yell or… something. Anything. Display her displeasure, her disappointment in some manner. Visidion stands next to her with his arms crossed over his chest staring between Drosdan and me. The tension in the room rises as the four of us stare, waiting for someone to speak or act. Minutes tick by but it feels like hours until at last I can't take it any longer.

"I'm sorry," I burst out.

"Sarah," Drosdan says, clenching my hand tighter.

"I'm sure you are," Rosalind says, and Visidion clears his throat.

Drosdan looks at Visidion, and something passes between the two Zmaj on a non-verbal level. Drosdan's shoulders slump and his tail goes still. His grip on my hand relaxes as his eyes drop down to stare at the bed.

"It all worked out," I say. "Gershom is dead. He was taking epis and went into withdrawal when he couldn't get any more."

"Idiot," Rosalind says.

"Yeah, well, that left his followers floundering. They were dying, so we had to save them."

"Did you?" Rosalind asks, arching an eyebrow.

"Yes!" I say. "We had to! I know you would have told me the same thing if you were there. We need them."

"Why didn't you bring them back to the City? I would have welcomed them here," she asks.

"They wouldn't," I say.

"You gave them a choice?" she asks.

That stops me. Swallowing hard, I think over my next words carefully.

"Yes," Drosdan interjects. "We did. We'd found a village that was in relatively good shape. I led them there."

"A village?" Visidion asks, speaking for the first time.

"One of the old mining communities," Drosdan answers. "There is water and buildings, enough for them to survive. They need to learn to hunt for food. I will help them."

"Will you?" Visidion asks.

Drosdan's wings rustle and his tail drags across the floor

back and forth as he squares his shoulders and meets Visidion's gaze.

"Yes, I will," he says, a finality to his voice.

He and Visidion match each other stare for stare.

"What happened to you?" Rosalind asks, ignoring the men as if nothing is happening.

"One of the guards," I say. "I didn't realize the situation had changed. Said something I shouldn't have."

Rosalind grimaces, shakes her head, and then sighs.

"Okay," she says, voice tight.

Her stare drills into me. Cold, hard, I've seen her do it so many times I thought I'd be immune to its effect but no such luck. Her face gives away nothing. Is she mad? Happy? Resigned?

"You made this decision on your own?" Visidion asks Drosdan.

The tension in the room keeps rising. The only sound between staccato delivered words is Drosdan's tail swishing across the floor. It's creating a pressure on my chest making it even harder to feel like I'm getting a full breath in. As if the broken ribs weren't problem enough.

"I have," Drosdan says.

"How many?" Rosalind asks.

"What?" I ask, tearing my eyes away from Visidion and Drosdan's confrontation.

"How. Many. Survivors?" she asks, emphasizing each word.

Blinking rapidly, I try to come up with an answer. Nothing. I don't know. How can I not know? She's trained me to observe everything. I collect data—it's what I do. My arms tingle, my breath comes in short gasps, my mind reaches for the information, but nothing comes. My mind is blank. Focus! I have to know this, of course I do. How can I not... and nothing.

"I… don't know," I say at last.

Rosalind sighs. "Of course."

Only now does she look away, turning to Visidion.

"We're done," she says.

Visidion doesn't look away from Drosdan but drops his arms to his sides and nods. The two of them turn in silence and walk towards the door. My heart pounds in my chest and an insane urge to laugh comes over me. This can't be it. It can't end like this. No, not like this.

"Wait!" I cry out, throat tight, mouth dry.

Rosalind stops, hand on the door, looking over her shoulder at me. My mouth moves, words should be coming out, but I'm blank, again. Emotions taking away every forming thought and leaving behind desperation and the need to say something, anything.

"Yes?" she asks, arching her eyebrow.

"It… can't…." Can't what? What do I say? How do I fix this? Grabbing Drosdan's hand in mine I squeeze it tight. "This is good!"

It blurts out without consideration. No thoughtful plan, no reasoning, but in my guts I know I'm right. I have to be. Rosalind looks at Visidion, and then as if they have some weird telepathic bond between them, they both turn, facing us. Rosalind looks imperious, the way she does to others. I've never been this to her. Outside, one of them, it leaves me cold, but behind that cold comes a certainty. She's trained me well. I've learned all her lessons, and I know, in the deepest parts of my heart, I know I'm right. I catch Drosdan's eyes and the moment passes between the two of us. We squeeze each other's hands. He is my rock. I am his treasure.

"How?" Rosalind asks, but I take the moment with Drosdan before answering so she continues. "How is it good that you two have allowed your base desires to destroy my entire plan for Gershom and his followers?"

"Gershom is gone," I say, sitting up straighter in the bed. "He openly plotted against you and you know it. He wanted power, no matter the cost, no matter who he hurt. Now that he's no longer influencing them, those who don't like the Zmaj will be less inflamed about it. They may not see reason, believe me they still don't like the Zmaj, but the blind hate is... less at least.

"Give them time. Help them, and they will become even more tolerant. They're in a village of their own now. Drosdan says it was a mining community. We can help them figure that out, reopen the mines. If we're going to grow, create the future that you see, we'll need more resources like that."

Rosalind's lips purse tight, the only sign on her face that she reveals, but something in her eyes shifts. I know her. She's been my mentor for years, and I know her better than anyone. I'm getting through to her. I also know when to shut up. She's thinking. Now is the point most people screw up with her. They take her silence as a void that needs filled and spew forth words that destroy their own argument. No, this is the time for quiet. Say nothing, wait for her question. Resist the urge itching inside to speak. It's a trick she taught me. People abhor a vacuum so they fill it with words, revealing more than any questions will ever get you.

"Okay," she says, nodding sharply. "Good work."

She turns again. I watch her leave with bated breath exhaling heavily only when the two of them are gone. The dam of tears I'd been holding back bursts, streaming down my face, and my breath comes in ragged gasps.

"Sarah," Drosdan says, taking me in his arms with his surprising gentleness.

He holds me like I'm a delicate piece of porcelain, which perhaps I am. In his arms, if nowhere else, I can be delicate. After all, I am his treasure.

21

DROSDAN

"I'm telling you I can't do it," Padraig says, snapping off each word and crossing his arms.

"And I'm saying I don't care what you can or can't do, do it," I reply, throwing my hands up.

"Look," Sarah says, stepping between the blacksmith and me. "They're going to need weapons if they're going to hunt for themselves. We can't be their main food supply."

Padraig doesn't take his eyes off me. His tail is still and his wings are partly open, and he leans in, openly challenging me.

"Not my problem," he says, his hands balling into fists as he drops his arms to his sides.

"I'm going to make it your problem," I snap, raising my tail.

My hearts pound loudly and my palms itch. I could tear him limb from limb, and I will if he doesn't do what I want.

"Wait!" Sarah exclaims, putting a hand on each of our chests.

I can't resist—my eyes dart to her. Padraig snorts, and the bijass floods my mind. I'm swinging before I can think to stop it. Sarah ducks as my fist connects with Padraig's jaw with a satisfying crack. He stumbles backwards, his hands flying up, his wings spreading, only his tail keeping him from falling down. Tools clatter to the ground as people drop what they are doing to watch.

"Damn it, Drosdan," Sarah exclaims, turning her full attention on me.

"What?" I say, shrugging.

Her upset cuts through the bijass, and in its wake I'm cold and empty. I can't meet her eyes, knowing for a moment I lost control. Padraig roars, taking a step towards me with his right arm cocked. Sarah stops him with a look and one finger in his face. He stares at the finger, arms dropping to his sides, tail hitting the sand.

"I—" he starts.

"No," she says emphatically. "Just no."

I can't stop the grin from forming until she whirls towards me as if she knew it, and her angry glare destroys all hints of amusement.

"No to you, too," she says, lips forming a tight, hard line.

I wonder how they would taste, and how long she could hold her serious look if I swept her into my arms and kissed her. I step towards her with every intention of following my urge, but she stops me by holding up an open hand and glaring. I throw my hands up in response. Becoming aware of how many members of the Tribe are watching right now, my scales warm in embarrassment. I'm the de facto leader with Visidion being over in the City, and I'm bending to Sarah like a plant bending to a sandstorm.

"Padraig, I know we don't have much in the way of resources for you to use, but the new village needs to be armed. We can't leave them out there without tools to fend for themselves," Sarah says.

"Can't do it," Padraig says, stubborn as a bivo. "I can barely supply us."

Sarah stares at him silently, waiting. Padraig meets her stare, and seconds crawl. He lasts longer than I expected, which I have to give him credit for, but he caves, dropping his eyes from hers.

"I thought so," Sarah says. "How long?"

"Spears by tomorrow," Padraig says, sullen. "No way in hell can I do lochabers for them."

"They don't need anything that fancy," Sarah says. "They'd only hurt themselves with weapons like that. Get the spears done. At least a dozen, okay?"

"Right," he says, walking away without a glance in my direction.

"Good, glad he's coming into line," I say.

"You," Sarah says, finger wagging under my chin. "Have to learn that not everything can be resolved with your fists."

"But—"

"No, no buts. We're better than that. We have to be. Rosalind and Visidion entrusted the Tribe to our care."

"Drosdan," Ragnar says, walking up with Olivia at his side, baby on her hip.

The baby clings to her blouse with the tiniest little hands I've ever seen. They're fascinating, so perfect and small. Each has a perfect, miniature fingernail on it that extends past the top of her fingers and comes to a small point, just like a full-grown Zmaj but minuscule. She shifts her grip, and her scales, subtle enough to almost miss, catch sunlight and sparkle like the rolling dunes out across the open fields.

"Drosdan, up here," Ragnar says, snapping his fingers in front of my face.

"What?" I snap, irritation flaring.

Soft cloth covers the baby's arm up to her tiny, sweet face. Full cheeks, almost as if they're stuffed with stored food, bright, sparkling blue eyes that match her mother's. Small nubs of horns, thin red hair growing right up to them without going past. She smiles and makes a gurgling sound. An odd emptiness echoes in my stomach, a void that needs to be filled.

"… Bashir will go to the village and stay—" Ragnar is saying.

"Huh? Stay?" I ask, shaking my head, trying to clear it of the baby. Ragnar, Olivia, Sarah, and the baby all stare at me, so I frown and cross my arms over my chest. "Fine."

"Two weeks," Olivia says. "He's not happy about it, but he's the best."

"Right, do it," I agree. "What do you mean he's not happy?"

Olivia and Ragnar exchange a look as the baby shifts its position, giggling, pulling my attention back to it like a magnet. What is wrong with me?

"He wants Penelope to come with him," Olivia says.

"We can't send her out there—she's heading up the garden and it's about to harvest!" I exclaim.

"Right," Ragnar says, looking past me at the green expanse growing out of the large cavern.

"Why would he want—?"

"Drosdan," Sarah cuts me off.

"What?" I ask. "We can't send her unless we can get Calista or Jolie here to oversee the harvest in her place. She knows more about it than anyone else. They're not going to leave the City without good reason. What is he even thinking? Why her?"

Past Sarah, I see Bashir next to the garden, standing inside the cavern. He turns and then I see that Penelope is with him. She touches his face, and he shakes his head. Understanding dawns.

"Oh," I say.

"Yeah," Olivia says.

"It's only a… short time," I say.

"So I've told him," Ragnar says. "He'll do it. He's loyal and a good man. It's not easy, though."

I know, better than most. I remember when Rosalind and Visidion sent Sarah off with Gershom. The pain I'd felt on finding out combined with anger, and then a long run across the desert. No matter, we do what we have to do.

"We can't send her, but who could we spare? Having a human with him would be smart anyway. They'll be nervous enough dealing with a Zmaj," I say.

"How about Delilah?" Sarah suggests.

"She was an engineer," Olivia adds. "Could be right up her alley to help if they do have a mine out there to get running."

"Good, see if she'll go," I say, pointedly not looking at the baby on her hip.

The baby's eyes are hypnotic—everything about her is tiny and perfect. She's a vacuum pulling me in, and I must resist. I don't understand what her pull on me is, or the way she makes me feel. It's a strange tingling that passes over my scales and settles into my core with an empty aching. I don't have time for this.

"I'll talk to Delilah," Olivia says. "First though, we haven't had time to properly introduce you."

"Introduce?" I ask, glancing at her quickly while carefully keeping my eyes off the baby and her strange gravity.

"Yes," Olivia says, her face beaming with a bright smile. "This is Zoe."

She lifts the baby up between us, holding her out towards me. Instinctively I reach out, then, gaining control of myself, I stop and put my hands back to my sides. What a fool I am to take such a tiny thing in my hands! How would I keep from damaging the child? She is too tiny for hands such as mine. I'm sure she's entirely too delicate. No, best to not touch.

Zoe gurgles, reaching her tiny arms out towards me. Minuscule fingers open and close, reaching... for me. My hearts pound in my chest, making it hard to breath. Can't get a deep enough breath. Light-headed. I'm swaying.

"Drosdan?" Sarah asks, resting her hand on my arm.

"I'm fine," I answer her, but my words are choked as I force them past the lump in my throat.

"It's okay," Olivia says. "I swear, you won't hurt her."

"Why would you think that?" I bark. Olivia laughs, and Ragnar is grinning from ear to ear. "I'm fine. She's just... I don't need to hold her right now. It's a pleasure to meet you, Zoe. I should be on my way."

"Drosdan," Sarah says, tightening her grip on my arm, stopping me from moving away.

"Drosdan," Ragnar says. "It's fine. I felt the same way, trust me. You won't hurt her."

Slowly I reach towards the small being, holding my hands out. Olivia lowers her into my hands. She's so small she fits in the palm of a single hand, but I don't risk that. I can't let her drop, can't apply too much pressure. She weighs nothing in my arms. Her sparkling blue eyes stare as if judging me, peering into my depths and deciding if I'm friend or foe. My shoulders are so tense it's making my head hurt. She turns her tiny head to the side, looking for her mother or father. Her tiny brow furrows, creating the smallest of wrinkles, then she looks back at me and smiles, showing her toothless gums. Tiny hands reach out towards me, and she coos a sweet, endearing sound.

The tension drains, and a strange sensation starts, like a fluttering in my stomach that sends tingles out through my limbs. Slowly, carefully, I bring the baby closer. Her smile widens, and she coos in what I think is pleasure. Holding her to my chest, the feelings explode in me, making it hard to breathe. It's as if my hearts are expanding until they don't want to fit in my chest. Glancing up, I see Sarah is watching, a big smile on her face. It hits me—this is what I want. Sarah and I should have a child of our own. A future opens up before me. One I hadn't considered possible. I'd given up on it so many years ago, since the devastation when all hope was lost.

"Hello," Sarah says, leaning over my arm and holding a finger out to the baby.

Zoe takes her finger and pulls it into her mouth, then starts sucking on it. I watch, unsure what to do now. Something moves against my hand. It takes me a moment to figure out that it's her tail. She's perfect, amazing, a stunning creation, and she, along with the other babies, is the future of both our races. Understanding comes with a rush, and for the first time I get what Rosalind is trying to do. Our races can't survive alone. We need each other. Zoe furrows her tiny brow, squints her eyes, then pulls Sarah's finger out of her mouth and cries. Even her cry is adorable, but cold fear pushes down the exhilaration in my chest.

"Okay," Olivia says, grabbing Zoe as if she is as sturdy as a sack of dried guster, and swings her up to her chest. "It's feeding time."

"She is okay?" I ask, hearts pounding.

"Sure, she's just hungry," Olivia says, obviously not concerned.

"Right," I agree, my arms feeling strangely empty. "So Bashir will go?"

I focus on Ragnar, trying to ignore the weird emptiness and ache in my chest and arms.

"Yes. Sending Delilah is good too," Ragnar says.

"We need a way to communicate," Sarah muses.

"What do you mean?" Ragnar asks.

"We're growing. When we were all in the City it wasn't a big thing, but now we're spread out. The Tribe here at the Caves, the City, now the Village or whatever name they give themselves. We need a method of communicating, something better than someone running days across the desert."

"How would we do that?" I ask.

"No clue," Sarah smiles. "It's just a thought."

"It would be helpful," Ragnar shrugs. "There used to be ways, I think, before."

Before. There were a lot of things, before. None of them are now. Now is all we have. Or is it? Sarah's smile, her bright sparkling eyes, the beautiful curve of her sweet lips. Before, there was no Sarah. There was no hope, but now she's here. Things change. No longer is anything set. We can change—everything can. Possibilities open up before us with every coming day. Olivia walks away carrying baby Zoe with her, and I know, with certainty, that the future is open now. Shifting sands out of which we can create anything we're willing to work hard enough to have.

"All right, make sure Bashir has all he needs. The Village needs our help sooner rather than later. We need to get food to them, and then train some of them to hunt on their own."

"I will," Ragnar says.

I turn in a slow circle, examining all we've accomplished here. When the Tribe arrived here, there was nothing more than a cliff. A rock jutting out of the rolling sand dunes thrust up in some long-ago upheaval. Dotted with small fissures and tiny caves, dominated by one large cavern leading into zemlja tunnels below the ground.

Now a stone wall arcs out from one end of the cliff and comes around to meet the far end, sealing off an open area of safety inside it. It makes this area defensible against both natural and unnatural threats. The majority of Tajss threats are held back by its presence alone. If any outside threat, such as the Zzlo attack again, it makes a defense against them possible. Inside the open area a market place has been established, pitched awnings covering carpets and shielding tables of goods from the direct light of the suns, running along the inside of the wall.

The fissures and tiny caves along the cliff have been opened and widened to create homes, and cloths now cover the openings, giving each group or family some privacy. The main cave now has a large garden emerging from its mouth. Irrigated by the water supply inside it through some creative engineering, a steady food source has taken shape. The human females work the garden every day in shifts, tending to the plants and making sure they are healthy and growing.

We've made a home.

Sarah puts an arm around my waist and leans her head on my chest.

"It's good," she says. "We've done well."

"Yes," I say, squeezing her tightly against me. "We have."

Satisfied I've done all I can for now, I move Sarah towards our own home. There are some basic needs of my own that want tending.

22

SARAH

*T*he suns create dancing rainbows as its beams bounce off Drosdan's scales.

Watching him standing on the walkway of the wall, staring out over the desert, my heart skips a beat. He's big, dominating, and he's mine. Every fiber of my being cries out for him. His touch, his love is the sustenance that I crave. He's like ice cream. Perfect, creamy, cold ice cream that quenches desire. Damn, I miss ice cream.

Shaking my head at the random thought, I walk down the ramp to the ground. Should I tell him now? It's still early, maybe too early to be sure, but I know. Deep in my heart, I know. A laugh cuts through my thoughts, and I glance to see Bailey and Ormarr through an open door. He touches her hand then quickly pulls back. Her cheeks flush bright red, and she looks swiftly away. Stopping in my tracks, I watch for a moment longer, but when it hits me I'm intruding on a private moment, I quickly move on.

Bailey and Ormarr? I wouldn't have... well why not? They're both healers, so I guess it makes sense. Age in a Zmaj is a relative thing, and Bailey is older, but that doesn't mean she doesn't need love, now does it? My smile takes over my face, and a spring comes into my step. Absolutely. They're perfect together. I'm really happy for her.

"Move that over here," Penelope's voice carries up the ramp.

I look down to where she's working in the garden, and I'm hit with a random wave of nausea. Closing my eyes, I focus on my breathing, pushing down the urge to empty my breakfast on the ground. A hot flash comes along with it, but panting my way past it helps.

"Are you okay?" Astrid asks,

When I open my eyes, she's standing too close. Nodding my head furiously, I continue focusing on my short breaths and controlling the nausea. Astrid shakes her blond hair, moving even closer, gripping me by both arms.

"You don't look okay."

"I know," I pant. "It's fine. Fine."

"Let me get Ormarr," she says.

Her grip is so strong—she has to be the strongest of all the women. Tall and curvy with a perfect build, she's as athletic as any girl could be.

"No," I say, gripping her back and stopping her from moving back up the ramp to where Ormarr and Bailey are.

The nausea passes and the heat of the flush fades.

"You're sure?" she asks.

"Yeah, there's nothing he can do about this right now," I say.

"Nothing he can do..." she trails off, tilting her head to the side. "Oh! You're—"

"Shhh!" I cut her off and look around to see if anyone heard her.

"Don't shush me, this is a good thing!" she says.

"Sure, but let me put it out there on my own," I shake my head. "I want to tell him myself."

"How far?" she asks, putting her hands on my stomach.

I've never felt more awkward in my life. I consider her a friend, but my friends don't normally grab my stomach, either. It's weird.

"Um, I... it's..." I stutter, trying to adjust to her hands moving across my belly as if it's not my own any longer.

"You can't be very far," she says. "You're barely showing, if at all."

"Six... weeks, I think," I manage to say at last.

"Oh! That's so exciting," she says, a wistfulness to her voice.

"Thanks," I say, and take a step back so her hands are no longer resting on me.

She doesn't seem to mind. Her grin is ear to ear.

"And I'm the first to know?" she whispers, leaning in conspiratorially.

"Um, yes," I say, trying to hide my disappointment at the fact.

I wanted to tell Drosdan first. It only seems right.

"Perfect," she says, looking over her shoulder. "You should tell him. He's going to be ecstatic."

"Yeah, I will," I say, feeling more and more awkward and out of place.

"You go, Momma," she says, slapping me on the ass as I walk away.

Wow, that was weird. Reaching the bottom of the ramps and making my way across the open area towards the wall, I see that Drosdan has just come down from the wall. Worry etches his face until his eyes land on me, and then a smile spreads across his face.

"My love," he says, running over and sweeping me off my feet.

His lips smash against mine as he twirls me around.

"Hi," I laugh when at last we part for air.

"You are my treasure," he says, kissing me again.

"I love you too," I say and he puts me gently back on my feet. "No sign of them yet?"

"Not yet," he says, mood turning somber.

"They'll be back," I say.

"Of course they will. It's probably taking longer to train them to hunt on their own," he says. "Bashir will be fine. He's an excellent hunter."

"Right," I agree. "Two weeks wasn't very long for him to train someone. Especially them, since they've got no skills to start with."

"I should have given them more time in the first place," he says. "Then I would not be worried."

"True, hindsight," I say. "But look, the first harvest is coming in nicely!"

We're walking past the garden, where most of the women are working on collecting the first full harvest since the project started.

"It's good," Drosdan smiles.

"That's not all that's good," I say, segueing in to what I really want to say.

"Of course not, you are all that is good in the world," he says and my heart soars at his words. His love envelops me as if it's a physical thing.

"I'm pregnant," I blurt out, I'd meant to say it softer, somehow couch it more carefully but it just flies out of my mouth.

"What?" he asks, stopping in his tracks, turning to me, eyes wide, mouth hanging open. "You're sure?"

"Yes," I say, nodding.

"YES!" he yells, his voice booming, echoing back to us off the rock cliff.

Everyone in the entire camp stops, turning to look at us. Warmth floods my cheeks, burning up my neck. He lifts me into the air, holding me at arm's length as if I weigh nothing, then lowers me down into a kiss. I'm stiff in his arms, too aware of the eyes on us. He breaks the kiss, still smiling.

"Well..." I say, trying to collect my thoughts.

He hooks his arm under my ass, cradling me in a carry, and runs. Bounding in leaps he runs halfway up the zig-zagging ramp that climbs the front of the cliff. He stops, puts me down, and faces the entirety of the Tribe, who are, for the most part, looking up at us now.

"We are pregnant!" he shouts. "A new child will join our Tribe! Blessings of water, I'm going to be a father!"

Cheers erupt, accented by applause. No matter how embarrassing it is, it's also welcoming. Warm and filled with love and support. This is my home. It may not be the way I ever thought my life would turn out, but it is, by far, better than anything I ever would have known on the ship. Drosdan turns me towards him and kisses me again. This time I give myself over to the kiss.

Tight coiling in my core makes a tightening need. Desire makes my heart race, pushing blood to my most sensitive parts. I'm wet and ready, aching with the need for him to fill me. It pushes past embarrassment, floods out any thought of being watched. I wrap my legs around his waist and let him carry me to our room. His massive, throbbing hard-on pushes against my pussy, striving to find its way past the confining clothes and into my wetness.

Whimpering in need, I thrust my hips back and forth, pressing him hard against my clit, finding some sweet release from the pressure there.

His tongue drives into my mouth in the same way I want his cock delving my depths. The change in brightness tells me we've entered our home. Pushing a hand between us, I loosen the tie of his pants, and pass my hand inside them. When I trail my fingers along his cock, he groans. I trace the edge of the head with a single finger, then slide my hand down the soft underside of his shaft.

After he sets me down, we throw clothes aside in a flurry, and he lays me down on our bed. Kissing his way down my neck and between my breasts, he buries his face in my pussy. Grabbing his hair, I thrust my hips up into him as his tongue digs through my soft, wet folds. He pushes his tongue into my tunnel, and I bite my lower lip, whimpering with pleasure. He drags his tongue up and grazes my clit, making me scream in pleasure as sensation overwhelms me.

Focusing his tongue on my hard nub, he circles and then presses hard against it. I'm pushed over the edge. Tightening my grip on his hair, I hold him there and circle my hips. Screaming his name over and over, my body is wracked by an intensity of pleasure that is too much. When it passes, I'm left a quivering mess. Muscles lax and not responding, I can barely keep my eyes open. Drosdan moves up over me, positioning his first cock at my opening.

As soon as his massive head touches my overly sensitive tunnel, I'm ready. There's an empty ache that only his cock will fill. Pressing into me, he moves slowly but I can't wait. Grabbing his hips, I pull up and thrust my hips forward at the same time, taking his massive, ribbed cock fully into my hot wet pussy in a single motion.

Once again I'm screaming his name in my pleasure. It's blindingly intense going from empty to fully filled in an instant. Distantly I hear him calling my name too, then we're thrusting. His cock drives in and out of me rapidly. There's no holding back. He pushes in and out faster, filling me over and over. Claiming me as I claim him. There's nothing to compare to the sensation.

He's mine as I give myself to him.

"Fuck me, Drosdan," I pant, pulling him in to me. "Take my pussy. You're mine."

He thrusts in and out with each syllable of every word. Giving himself to me fully until I feel his cock swelling inside me, and I know he's close. I thrust into him hard, one hand on his toned ass and the other tangled in his hair, holding myself tight against him as I feel his cock spasm over and over, dumping his fresh seed into me.

My pussy clamps onto his cock as it starts pushing his load. Holding onto him, milking it, taking all that he has to give as an electrical storm plays through my body. I've never, even with him, felt as satisfied as I do now. Knowing that the life we have created is growing inside me somehow makes this more intense. It's a celebration not only of each other, but of life. A recognition of a future we didn't know we would have.

He moans my name as his cock spasms one last time, then I feel it softening. Slowly he pulls out, lying down next to me. I turn my head to him and we kiss. Soft, gentle kisses. The primal intensity has subsided for the moment. His fingers trace circles across my body as we stare into each other's eyes.

"You're happy?" I ask.

"More than I ever imagined I could be," he replies.

"Good," I say, glancing down to see his second cock rising.

"Seems we have more to do?" I ask, teasing as I trace the ridges of it.

"Only if you're ready," he says, moaning softly with eyes half-closed.

"Always, for you, my love. Always."

THE END

———————————

Did you enjoy *Dragon's Desire?* Be sure to leave a review! It's the best way for you to help me as a self-published author.

Keep reading for a special sneak peek at
Night of the Dragons

EXCLUSIVE PREVIEW: NIGHT OF THE DRAGONS

PIPER

The four enormous alien dragon-men stand there for a few more seconds, until I wonder if that's all they want to do, just stand and watch, and if they expect me to just keep floating and let them. But then they all move towards the water, almost in unison, their eyes locked on me. My heartbeat picks up even more, and I feel completely exposed. Being naked makes me feel more vulnerable than ever, even though, realistically, I was always vulnerable around them.

I turn my head, trying to see them all at once, though I can't when they're coming from every direction it seems like. From my front, my sides, behind me. One of them alone would be intimidating, just with his massive size. Four is overwhelming as they near me. As they hit the water, kilt-like cloths swirl around their muscled, bulky thighs, the water level rising up their legs. It's a low shallower for them than it is for me.

Then they're right up next to me, surrounding me on every side, a wall of muscle. It seems to be their favorite position. Maybe they like cornering me. I shiver as they growl softly, each pair of eyes I meet filled with a carnal heat that has tingles spreading through my body, the edge of danger only adding to my arousal. I also really wish I could just close my eyes and disappear. Go figure. But the two conflicting feelings exist side by side. The situation is just so out of my experience, my comfort zone. It hits my buttons, but it also feels like a bad idea, like it could get out of hand quickly.

And then it escalates. I'm not in that position for long. Fire picks me up easily, pressing me against his hard, cool front. I automatically raise my legs to wrap them around his waist to stabilize myself, my hands sliding onto his broad shoulders so I don't fall. I gasp as I feel the ridiculously large erection rub up against me, with only the thin, almost transparent cloth of his kilt-like covering between us. There may as well be nothing at all there, that cloth is so thin and wet. I can feel him pulsing against me in his excitement, feel exactly how thick and long he is. And it doesn't leave me unaffected.

I groan, heat and a warm tension clamping down in my belly at the feel of him. Between my thighs. I'm panting softly as I marvel at how his proximity is affecting me. I've never felt this kind of mind wiping arousal, the kind that pushes my inhibitions aside, makes my self-consciousness fade against the face of it. Even as a voice tells me in the back of my head to be careful, that I don't really know any of these men, that I don't know what to expect, all I want to do is move my body against his. Feel more of this insanity. Rub against that ridiculous erection where it throbs against me. I can't focus on anything but that driving need.

I make a small, involuntary sound as I try to rub myself against that hard length, needing more than the press of him against me, staring into his pretty amber eyes, his handsome face softening at the touch. At how it makes him feel.

Four identical, frustrated growls sound from around me as they see me trying to slide against him. And then I'm suddenly torn right out of Fire's arms and into someone else's, the loss of his hard length from between my legs making me cry out in protest. I might have to get used to being pulled away from each of them. It seems to be how they operate.

I get a brief glimpse of Emerald before he closes the distance between our faces and settles his mouth against mine. He doesn't hold back or beat around the bush at all. Not that he needs to with how hot I'm already feeling. The kiss goes from zero to a hundred so fast my head is spinning while I try to gasp in a breath. His tongue slides against mine. His taste is seductive, his lips moving firmly, mobile and confident against my mine as he explores my mouth. I sink into that kiss, feeling the heat build even more at the contact. And now all I can think about is Emerald, his hard body against mine, the pretty yellow-and-green of his scales. The equally impressive erection pressed against my belly.

How can I just go from man to man like this and enjoy each one so much? But how am I supposed to resist such sexy men when they all want me so badly? I don't have much time to dwell on that thought or to enjoy Emerald either.

Another pair of hard arms flips me around in Emerald's hold. And now it's Danger staring at me, his eyes filled with an intense heat. My breath catches as I meet those eyes. I feel like he might be able to burn me with that look alone, it's so searing. His piercing gaze is so focused, I wonder if he can see exactly what I'm thinking, how hot the situation is making me. Despite how hot that look is, he doesn't pull me away from Emerald like I expect him to, like everyone else seems to like to do. Instead, he presses me back against Emerald, my back against his friend's solid chest.

He lifts my legs so that I wrap them around his narrow waist, suspending me between the two of them. I'm completely naked with nobody's body to obstruct the view of mine. It sends another bolt of fire through me. Oh, I feel much more open and vulnerable now. They can all see everything. Danger can see everything.

My eyes lock on his face as his drift down to my body, taking in every inch slowly, not rushing. Taking his time to look. I have the urge to cover myself, but I can't in this position. So I just watch him, my breath coming faster as his large hands smooth up the length of my legs. Up my shins. My thighs. My hips. Across my stomach. I look down to see the stark contrast of his dark, strong hands against my pale, much more delicate skin, the arresting sight holding my attention. He touches me slowly, sensually. As if he could do it all day and not tire of it. Feeling so wanted is an aphrodisiac all on its own, isn't it? I didn't realize that until now.

I almost forget Emerald is there because I'm so focused on what Danger is doing. Until he reaches around me to cup my breasts, squeezing the soft mounds gently in his cool hands. Pinching my already hard nipples between his teasing fingers. I arch at the sharp sensation, the feeling sending an answering warmth between my legs.

That's when one of Fire's hands finally moves between my legs, where I can feel the heat gathering, pooling as my excitement grows. His fingers slide through my folds, exploring, touching every inch of me gently, my own slickness helping him glide across. Well—touching almost every inch. There's one in particular that he stays away from, much to my frustration. He deliberately teases me, rubbing on either side of my clit, smoothing his hand just above, teasing my entrance with a fingertip below. He never quite touches me there directly, where I'm throbbing with the need to be caressed.

I moan as Royal strokes my face lightly, leaning down to whisper in my ear. His low, husky voice sends shivers down my spine, his hot breath sending goosebumps down my neck. I can't understand a word of what he's saying. But it's still fucking sexy. The tone, the desire in it, the thread of demand. Yeah. I don't know what he's saying, but I really wish I did.

I open my eyes slightly as they continue to tease me, feeling almost drugged by the sensations overtaking my body. They lap at me as gently as the water around us, just as all-encompassing.

My eyes move to Fire's intense gaze as he steps back. Watching. His abs are clenched, his muscles standing out, every strong inch of his torso on display, wet with water. My eyes slowly slide down his body, the muscles there rippling as he moves his arm rhythmically. That's when I notice his hands are now under the water. I can't quite see them from this angle. But there's no mistaking the jerking motion of his forearm. He can only be doing one thing.

Another bolt of arousal shivers through my body at the realization. I lick my lips as I raise my eyes back to his, scanning all that smooth skin, wishing I could see his hand wrapped around his erection too. See how he likes it. How hard he's squeezing his cock. When I reach his face, he's still watching me as he touches himself, his eyes mesmerizing in their lust. I can't look away from the heat there, from the driving need that I can sympathize with.

Even as Danger's hands drive me right to the edge and no further. Coming so close to where I want him to touch me. I can't take it anymore. I can't.

"Please," I murmur, trying to move my hips towards his clever fingers, trying to get them where I want them. I know he can't understand my words, but I know he can understand my body, how it's moving against him, and the fact that I'm now unashamedly begging for what I want. For what I need. There's no room for shame, not with the way I need it.

"Please," I moan again, my nails digging into the back of

his neck, into his shoulder, skating the gorgeous, sharp edge of oblivion.

Please.

NIGHT OF THE DRAGONS
is available now on Amazon

ABOUT THE AUTHOR

USA Today Bestselling Author of fantasy and scifi romance, Miranda Martin's books feature larger than life heroes with out-of-this-world anatomy and smart heroines destined to save the world. As a little girl she would sneak off with her nose in a book, dreaming of magical realms. Today she brings those fantasies to life and adores every fan who chooses to live in them for a while.

She was born and raised in southern Virginia, but as a veteran she's traveled to places like Korea, Hawaii and good 'ole Texas. Now she's settled in Kansas, the heart of America, with her husband and daughters. Her favorite animals are dragons, unicorns and cats. If she's not writing, you can still find her tucked away somewhere with a warm blanket and her nose in a book.

Get in touch!
mirandamartinromance.com
miranda@mirandamartinromance.com

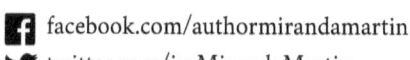
facebook.com/authormirandamartin
twitter.com/imMirandaMartin
instagram.com/imMirandaMartin

ALSO BY MIRANDA MARTIN

Red Planet Dragon's of Tajss Series
Red Planet Jungle Series
The Power of Twelve Series
The Alva Series
Dragon's & Phoenixes Series